Sing Me a Lullaby

Kerry Christine Vrossink

BALBOA.
PRESS

A DIVISION OF HAY HOUSE

Balboa Press books may be ordered through booksellers or by contacting:

Balboa Press
A Division of Hay House
1663 Liberty Drive
Bloomington, IN 47403
www.balboapress.com.au
1 (877) 407-4847

Because of the dynamic nature of the Internet, any web addresses or links contained in this book may have changed since publication and may no longer be valid. The views expressed in this work are solely those of the author and do not necessarily reflect the views of the publisher, and the publisher hereby disclaims any responsibility for them.

The author of this book does not dispense medical advice or prescribe the use of any technique as a form of treatment for physical, emotional, or medical problems without the advice of a physician, either directly or indirectly. The intent of the author is only to offer information of a general nature to help you in your quest for emotional and spiritual well-being. In the event you use any of the information in this book for yourself, which is your constitutional right, the author and the publisher assume no responsibility for your actions.

Any people depicted in stock imagery provided by Thinkstock are models, and such images are being used for illustrative purposes only. Certain stock imagery © Thinkstock.

Print information available on the last page.

ISBN: 978-1-5043-1185-4 (sc)
ISBN: 978-1-5043-1184-7 (e)

Balboa Press rev. date:12/18/2017

Synopsis

Cassandra Nelson is a woman with only one ambition, to be a Mother. Fate however, is not on her side. Divorced from her first husband because of his sterility, she sets out to find a man who can father her child.

Jake Marshall is that man. With four children living with him from his previous marriage, his own Market Garden and a comfortable home in the northern suburbs of Perth, it seems a Higher Force is smiling at her. The only obstacle however, is Dane Marshall, the oldest of the four. He is determined to rid her from his Fathers' life, and her battle to be accepted by him finally comes to a crux when she is pushed down a flight of stairs while pregnant at last with her own child; causing her to give birth at 20 weeks premature. Not only does her baby die, she must have a hysterectomy. This sends Cassie spiraling into the realms of the insane and into the arms of her best friend's husband. Her obsession for having a child is suddenly turned into a vehement need for revenge.

Slowly all but one of Jake's children die through strange accidents and his misery deepens he seeks solace with his ex wife Rae.

While his ex father in law, Sergeant Carl Barrett, tries to fathom out the mode of his grandchildren's demise, it seems Cassis' revenge is working out for her. And now the sweetest of them all, is seeing Dane punished for his atrocities.

Prologue

Dane Marshall sat rigidly, turning occasionally to peer at the throng of people gathering slowly into the Courtroom. Some he knew, most he didn't. The sadistic media were poised, cameras ready, just waiting to immortalize his face when the verdict was passed down.

His wispy blonde fringe hid the beads of perspiration that had collected on his brow, while his sea green eyes tried unsuccessfully to conceal the terror that ravaged his body, and blink away the brine from his sweat, or was it tears? He felt like a child at school waiting in the principal's office for ten of the best ones across his palms, but then he was a child, wasn't he? At 18 some would see him as a delinquent erred along the passage of youth, but most, *she*, would class him as nothing less than a cold blooded murderer, the savage beast who took the life of his younger siblings.

If the verdict was not guilty he would be set free to continue his life as a normal human being, but he knew without doubt he would be ostracized by his Father and friends, he would have to make a life elsewhere possibly away from Australia the Country he loved. However, should the verdict go the other way, he would be caged like an animal for the rest of his life only to be slain by his inmates at the first opportunity.

Glancing towards the blank expressionless face of his Father, his eyes accidently locked with the steel gaze of pale sapphires, the eyes of his stepmother. Her blue black hair captured severely in a chignon made her appear older than her 31 years. The small red mouth was turned slightly at the corners, sneering at him. It was all *her* fault. If she hadn't married his Father four years ago, he wouldn't be sitting here now, squirming in this chair feeling the warm dampness spreading slowly between his legs.

Ten years younger than his Father she had made life hell for all of them; always sneaking into his bedroom and rummaging through his drawers looking for the drugs she was convinced he had; telling them off for doing things that their Father had always allowed. This woman was nothing but trouble, he knew it, his Grandfather knew it and his Mother knew it. His Mother … his heart filled with sadness at the thought of her. All this had been too much for her to endure. She had fought desperately for his innocence, but all evidence lead to him, there was not one single thing that could be traced to Cassie, and finally through shear frustration his Mother had had a nervous breakdown, and now sat rocking pathetically in a hospital. It had been hard enough for her trying to accept the accidental death of Carly, then a short time later Felicity and then finally Jeffrey. And now this: she would never recover and it was all that *bitchs'* fault, it should be her lying in the cemetery and one day somehow, he would put her there.

A voice from beyond brought him back to the present, "All rise," the Judge and Jurors were coming back in. His six week trial was about to end, and more than likely, so was his life. He glanced at his Lawyer on his right, who was staring sightlessly at his notes. This stony faced wimp was only there as a symbol. He had pegged him guilty from beginning and had gone through the motions of defense as though it were a second rate play. He had been appointed by the Court, it was a job, and he drew the same salary whether he won or lost.

Dane rose slowly conscious of the smell of incontinence and the dampness visible on his crotch. He could feel his Stepmother's eyes boring into his skull, she would be smiling openly; she had won. He knew; they all knew what the verdict would be.

Chapter 1

The music blared, bouncing loud decibels through her eardrums, reverberating into a thunderous headache. Touching her escort (or rather pickup) on the arm, she stood up and gestured to leave.

The young man glanced up and flashed his large, white teeth then shook his head, the tight, dark curls that surrounded his oval chubby face dancing in tempo with the rest of his anatomy. He was having a good time and had no intention of leaving, especially since he knew he had no chance of scoring with her.

Cassandra Nelson shook the long, black mane that appeared blue under the heavy lights of the nightclub, shrugged her slender shoulders, and walked out. It was no big deal. She had come alone and she would leave alone, so what? He was a jerk anyway—only after one thing.

As soon as his sweaty, little hand inched slowly along her leg to her thigh, she knew he was just like the rest. *One day,* she thought, *one day I'll meet the right man.* She chuckled to herself as the image of her tall, dark knight in shining armour dissipated into the short, stout jerk she had just left.

Climbing into her small red Cortina, she decided in the future she would be more selective about the men she allowed to pick her up. Winding the window down, she edged slowly along the highway, allowing the cool breeze to caress her face and blow away the effects of the hot January day and stifling evening. Glancing at her watch, she sighed. It was only 12:30 a.m. There was an old hotel on the next corner that stayed open until 2:00, so she decided to call in and have a very dry martini before going home to her depressing three-room unit.

As she turned into the driveway, a sudden flash of white lunged then rolled towards her. Instantly hitting the brakes, the car lurched then veered to the right, stopping inches from a light pole. *Shit! What the hell was that?*

With her stomach still high in her throat, she jumped out and raced over to where a man lay in the centre of the road. His white shirt, ragged and torn, was soaked with fresh blood. Her head pounding and spinning, she felt for a pulse. *I didn't hit him. I'm sure I didn't. There was no bump, no thud.* Her mind was in turmoil. At that moment, his bearded mouth opened and he grunted. The strong stench of alcohol on his breath reeked, bringing her hand to cover her nose.

"Don't worry about Jake, lady. He's as drunk as a skunk."

Cassie turned to face a large, burly man, arms folded, who was propped in the doorway of the hotel. "You didn't hit him; he was thrown out by the scruff of his neck. Best thing you could do is roll him in the gutter and go on to wherever you're going."

His nonchalant tone irritated her. "But the blood," she said.

"He was in a fight. Reckoned one of the guys rolled him and started throwing his fists around."

"Can't you put him a taxi and send him home?"

"Nope! I don't waste my time with scum like him. Ever since his wife had the good sense to divorce him, he's been hanging around here making a nuisance of himself. If you want to take him home, that's your business, but he lives way out in Wanneroo so you'd be sending good money after bad as far as I'm concerned."

Cassie had moved to Western Australia from Melbourne only three months before, but she knew Wanneroo was clear across Perth. "I don't get it. Why does he drink here in Victoria Park when he lives way out there?" she queried.

"Cause his ex drinks here sometimes so he hangs around hoping to see her, I guess. Like I said, if you want to take him home, that's up to you, but I'm not responsible for his pile of crap parked out the back. So if it's gone in the morning …" He shrugged. "Well, then it's gone. Personally, I would throw him in it and let him sleep it off, although this isn't the best area to be sleeping in a car."

He turned to the left and spat up a ball of mucus from his throat. "Up to you, lady. Do whatever you want."

She looked at this disgusting man with disdain. "Can you at least *help* me put him in my car?"

He shrugged and said, "Sure."

Cassie once again looked at him in disgust, then back to the pitiful creature on the road. It was at least a forty-five-minute drive and she had just a quarter tank of fuel. And since she'd just spent her last twenty dollars on that waste of space back at the nightclub … "Oh boy. I haven't any money to get fuel," she whispered. A thought occurred. "Could you check his pockets and see if he has any money?"

"He's already used all his cash in there," the large, burly man said as he pointed back to the pub, "which is why I asked him to leave so politely."

"OK. Well then, I don't suppose you could either lend me some money to get fuel?"

He let out a loud hysterical laugh. "Are you kidding, lady? Firstly, I don't know you from Eve. And secondly, I don't know his actual address. Only Wanneroo. Like I said, leave him in his car."

"You're a real humanitarian, I can tell! Thank you for nothing. Now if you could just help me get him in my car."

Without hesitation, this balding, grotesque man bent over the semi-conscious man, grabbed him by the shoulders, and literally threw him across his own broad shoulders with as much ease as it would take her to lift a baby. "Open the back door and I'll toss him in."

Cassie watched in horror as he did exactly that. There was no gentleness about this mountain of a man, and she made a mental note not to ever cross the path of this creep again.

It was only a five-minute drive to her flat, during which her passenger managed to throw up twice. Turning right off the highway, the tall building containing hers and sixty other flats rose ominously against the stars. Cassie hated this building. It reminded her of something you'd find in a horror movie. But it was cheap and money—or rather the lack of— was her downfall. One stroke of good luck: at least she had a ground-floor unit.

She turned into the drive then drove across the lawn to her front door, daring not to think what Mr. Tyson, the caretaker, would say if he saw where she was parked. As she stepped from the car, she tripped over a sprinkler and fell heavily to her knees. "Shit! This is what I get for being a good Samaritan!"

A thought suddenly occurred. "Oh crap. Please don't let me be parked on any of his damn sprinklers, or I'll be out on my ear tomorrow," she prayed while getting to her feet.

Opening the back door, she pulled Jake—was that what the bully bouncer called him?—to a sitting position. Fortunately, he was of a reasonably slim build and not too heavy, so she was able to manoeuvre one of his arms across the back of her neck. Holding him tightly around the waist and grabbing his flaying hand, she managed to half walk and half drag him to the front door. Propping him against the door, she fumbled with the lock and cursed, "Why the hell didn't I open the bloody door first?"

Finally, she heard the familiar click but was unprepared for what happened next. Jake felt the door give way, through blurred vision saw a shape, and reached instinctively for it. Cassie was suddenly jerked by the neck and began to fall. Within a split second, she was down, her head hitting the sparsely covered concrete floor in the living room, his dead weight on top of her. The vile smell of beer and sick hung heavily around him.

With the acute pain in her thumping head, she lay stunned, swallowing the desire to throw up.

It was a full minute before she had the strength to push him off. He lay in a deep sleep. "*Bastard*," she muttered as she sat up, trying to control the waves of nausea.

It took a further five minutes before she was steady enough on her feet to make the effort to repark her car in her personal bay.

Cassie rose and showered at around ten the next morning. There was a distinctive "egg" on the back of her head, a very sore reminder of her one and only good deed. Her flat, which was comprised of lounge-dining, kitchen, bedroom, and bathroom, still held the unforgettable odour of her guest. He lay in the same position on the floor she had left him, arms folded across his chest like a corpse. He had snored profoundly most of the night, and Cassie, weary from lack of sleep, couldn't resist the urge to give him a gentle kick in the side. It took several more kicks before Jake broke his sleep. His eyes widened in awe at the vision of the tall, dark-haired woman dressed in jeans and sweatshirt gazing down at him. Temporarily dumbfounded, he continued to stare, his stomach churning precariously and his entire body in one massive pain.

Cassie finally broke the silence. "Well, Jake, I won't ask how you feel this morning; the green tinge around your mouth speaks volumes."

He tried to smile his embarrassment away, but his mouth hurt and he winced at the effort. "I'm afraid, miss, you have the advantage."

"Here, let me help," she stated as he attempted to sit up. "I'm Cassandra Nelson—Cassie if you like—and I almost ran over you in the early hours of this morning."

He accepted her outstretched hand graciously.

"Thanks. Are you sure you didn't I feel as though I was hit by a truck!"

"I believe 'the truck' was in fact someone's fist."

Jake rubbed his jaw, "Oh yes, that's right. I think I may have made an ass of myself last night at Tony's."

"I suppose that's one way of putting it. Would you like some coffee and I'll fill you in on just how much of an ass you were."

His only comment as she relayed the events as she knew it, was an occasional 'oh dear'. "You mean I was literally tossed onto the road in front of you."

Her small well shaped mouth quivered slightly, obviously trying not to laugh, "Yes, and if I'd been going 1 Kilometer faster, you would have spent last night in the morgue." He looked into her lucid blue eyes and noted the amusement.

"Well I'm certainly pleased that my almost demise amuses you," he stated dryly. She was matronly attractive with her hair drawn severely to the back, not exactly beautiful but lovely nevertheless, and the strange stirring in his stomach was not through alcohol.

"Not exactly Jake: to be perfectly honest, you frightened the crap out of me; it was the horrified look on your face earlier that I find comical. It was the look of a man caught with his pants down in a shop window," she giggled.

He thought about it for a moment, the picture of how he must have looked to her formed in his mind, and he tried unsuccessfully to smile once more. "Yes well, I thank you sincerely for your kindness and coffee, and shall be on my way." He stood to leave, and grimaced as the sudden movement lanced his head with pain. Cassie stood with him, noting his discomfort, "just give me a moment to put my shoes on, and I'll give you a lift back to your car." Jake almost accepted her offer. The chance to spend a few more minutes with her was so tempting, but then reason interceded, she most likely considered him a real no hoper and couldn't wait to see the back end of him; he shook his head, "No; please, I don't want to impose a moment longer."

"It's no imposition really, it's only five minutes up the road, and it won't take long at all." For a moment, he thought he almost detected a note of disappointment in her response, but then his head was still fuzzy with the after effects of the night before, so it was probably more his imagination than anything else. "In that case, I will certainly walk back to Tony's. It will do me the world of good; give me a chance to clear my head. Just point me in the right direction."

She smiled with understanding, "Sure, that way," she gestured with her head, but as she felt his presence diminish, she felt a peculiar sense of regret.

Chapter 2

Jake Marshall walked slowly towards the Pub. Holding his head high he ignored the curious glances of passersby at his disheveled appearance. This was the last time he was going to be caught in this predicament. Never again would he hang around the sleazy pub that stayed open when all others had closed. If he was to be honest with himself, he knew Rae wouldn't darken the door of any establishment he attended. *It was over*! There, he'd finally admitted it, it was over. Shaking his head with new found determination, he made a silent pledge to put more effort into his as yet unsuccessful market garden, and spend a lot more of his leisure time at home with his four children. Jake realized they missed a Mother's influence, so from now on he would do his damndest to adopt both roles.

Sergeant Carl Barrett sat behind his mahogany desk, his grey eyes following the young Constable through the glass partition. He was entering his office, but didn't need to speak; Carl could read his face, "Don't tell me, another one?" The young officer nodded, "Where?"

"Car park at MacDonald's. Head bashed to a pulp. All evidence indicates she was sexually assaulted, and Serg …" Carl's eyes showed no expression as he waited for the impending news. "She was only 12 or 13!"

"*DAMN IT*!" His fist hit the desk hard, the coffee he had recently poured spilled steaming into his lap. "Fu.." he caught his tongue as a policewoman entered at that precise moment. "*WHAT DO YOU WANT*!?" he bellowed. She pushed her hair further under her cap and sighed. This was not the first time he had roared at her and whereas once it would have sent her quivering from his office, now she shrugged it off as just another one of his 'bad days'.

"I've just had another phone call from Gordon Eastway over at Tony's. It seems Jake's been fighting with his patrons again.

"*So!*" he snapped, his face a bloodless mask of anger and frustration.

"So, he said if you don't do something about him, he is going to bring the roof down, and make life a misery for you."

"I'm not that idiot's bloody keeper and my bloody life is already a misery! Jake Marshall is nothing but a drunken bum and since my daughter divorced him, he is not my responsibility. What does that moron Eastway expect me to do, cuff Jake to his bloody bed every night?"

Two blank faces stared at him. Jake had been a thorn in his side from the day he married Rae and it was obvious things hadn't changed much. He sighed heavily "all right, all right. I have to go home and change my pants anyway; I'll call in and see Rae on the way. Maybe she can talk some sense into that idiot."

Rae Barrett Marshall lived in a small unit in Shenton Park, three streets away from her parents. Since her divorce she had seen her children only four times, mainly because Jake had been unable to accept their marriage failure, placing the blame in her direction, making her feel guilty and consequently turned each visit into a sparring match.

Trying to mould her career as an artist wasn't easy, she found herself skimping and scraping on more occasions than she cared for. For this reason she knew taking custody of her children at this stage at least, would be futile and most definitely not in their best interest. She was standing at her easel in front of the window when her father pulled up. The door opened before he reached the step; "Hello precious," he smiled affectionately and tried to ignore the fact that at 11:45a.m. She was still in her dressing gown.

"Hi Dad," she kissed him lightly on the cheek and stepped aside allowing entry into the modest living room. He moved to the easel, the canvas blank.

"Not doing too well honey?"

"No, I just can't seem to get into it these days. Want some coffee Dad?" Glancing down at the stain on his lap, he declined.

"Rae, why don't you pick up the children and move in with your Mother and me? I can't stand seeing you living in this matchbox, besides children *should* be with their mother."

This conversation was becoming tiresome, she sighed, "Dad, we've been over this time and time again. I have to do this on my own. As soon as I start making some decent money I'll rent a house and file for custody, but not before then."

"It's not easy trying to build a career from a hobby Rae. There's a position open at the station for a filing clerk and I've been holding it for you. Now the money's not terrific mind, but it is regular and would tide you over until you can get further established with your art. What do you say?"

Sitting on the faded and cracked second hand leather lounge, she folded her hands behind her short blonde hair. Smiling hazel eyes sparkled with affection for her well rounded Father, who of late, reminded her of Cannon. His grey eyes seemed almost hidden by his protruding forehead, while full rosy cheeks drooped like a basset hound which quivered like jelly whenever he laughed. The receding hair line seemed to have been white forever and at only fifty seven, she knew he must have grayed prematurely, most likely brought on by the stress of his work. She had been his 'precious' and 'honey' for thirty four years, yet these terms of endearment still made her feel special.

"Dad I love you and I appreciate the fact that you're worried about me, but I am not cut out to be a clerk. I want to paint"

Carl moved to the window, "You have to be dead before it does you much good honey."

Rae shrugged, "So my kids will benefit. I'll be happy just earning enough to pay the bills, and quite candidly, I don't particularly care what happens after I'm dead."

"Alright I get your point, but what's wrong with accepting the position at the station and paint in your spare time, then when you start selling your work, you can quit." He had crossed his arms and was rocking back and forth on his heels, a habit Rae detested intensely. Pulling back her hair, she yawned;

"Dad, you and I both know the position you're talking about is one you'd conveniently make the day I started. I'm sorry you don't approve, but this is what I want to do, so please just let me do it my way."

Carl had to concede. It was true there was no job on hold, but he hadn't thought she would see through him so quickly, but then, wasn't she a Sergeant's daughter and from a toddler she'd been taught to read between the lines. Obviously he had taught her well. "Alright I'll stop hounding you."

"Thank you. Now you can tell me the real reason you're here." He tried to look surprised and hurt, then realized she had read him again and sighed, "Jake." Her face changed to disapproval, she didn't want to talk about him.

"Really, what's he done now," her tone was casual, uncaring.

"Nothing too serious really, he's been fighting at Tony's again. Is there anyway, you could talk him into keeping his drinking under control?"

Rae frowned, she found the subject of her ex husband extremely distasteful. "He's a grown man Dad, what he does is his business, and he certainly wouldn't listen to me. Have you forgotten one of the reasons for our divorce was lack of communication, so what hope do you think I'd have now?"

Carl moved to her, crushing her fine build against him, in a bear like embrace. "I hear you precious, but won't you try, for me. Even though I loathe the man, I don't want to have to arrest my ex son in law for being drunk and disorderly. It would ruin my image, if you know what I mean."

Slight tremors erupted within his grasp; her head was bobbing up and down catching his chin softly. Taking a step back, he held her at arm's length; she was trying not to double up with laughter. It took a moment before she was composed enough to speak, "All right Dad, for you I'll try; but I can't guarantee anything." A second series of chuckles radiated forth, she eased herself back into his arms, where her contagious mirth took effect. Within seconds, she could feel her father's large stomach begin to shake as he joined in her laughter.

Cassie watched from the front door until Jake disappeared around the corner. Once closed, she turned and crossed to the bedroom where she removed a small note book from her dressing table drawer, and began to write: 12th Jan, 1984. "I thought I had killed a man this morning. He was literally thrown in front of my car by this hideously creepy man. His name is Jake and it's a shame I didn't meet him under different circumstances, perhaps we could have been friends."

Two weeks later she left Darcy's, the store where she worked selling shoes, to meet her best friend Philyce Dantry in a hotel in Tuart Hill for a few drinks. Normally only a twenty minute drive from the City, this evening the 6:00pm traffic was particularly hectic and it took fifty minutes. Cassie was blazing when she finally arrived, then after waiting a further thirty minutes realized she had been stood up.

Snatching her hand bag, she stood and tightened the wide black belt that encased her small waist. There was a man standing at the bar staring at her, his green eyes almost daring her to speak. Well she would certainly do that in no uncertain terms. She was in too much of a bad mood to be picked up tonight and she would tell him so. As she approached, her small breasts heaving in anger beneath the pink cotton dress, he smiled. Something was familiar about him, but she couldn't remember what.

"Hello Cassandra Nelson, you look like a lady in distress."

Cassie searched his face carefully, she recognized his face, but where; when; he laughed softly, "Now I have the advantage it seems."

"Well for goodness sake, if it isn't my star boarder, err.., Jake, right?"

He nodded and rubbed his chin. "Ah ha, you shaved off the beard, that's why I didn't recognize you, she remarked."

"It's part of my new image, what do you think?" Giving him the once over, she nodded with approval. He was rather good looking without the fuzz surrounding his mouth, and his tight jeans and open shirt exposing a handful of blonde hair, stirred a rather pleasant feeling in her stomach.

"Yes, you scrub up rather well."

"Can I buy you a drink, or are you in a hurry to leave?" He tried to sound casual, but she picked up the note of hopefulness and blushed slightly, "Sure, why not. I was only going home. I'll have what you're having."

He raised an eyebrow, "Well it's only soda water I'm afraid; not very interesting."

"That's OK I'm driving anyway."

An hour later Cassie found herself wanting to keep the evening alive and before realizing it, she had invited him back to her flat for a late dinner. Jake looked at his watch, he had told Skye his babysitter he would be home by 8 and it was already 8:30. He should go, but he was enchanted by her charisma and wanted to stay.

"Excuse me a moment, I have to make a quick call."

A thousand butterflies began a slow rhythm in her stomach. What if he had someone waiting at home for him? Not that it was any of her business but she had no intention of inviting a man back to her house if he was already in a relationship. When he returned a moment later, she spoke openly. "You don't by any chance have a wife or girlfriend waiting somewhere in the background do you, because if so, you may as well know I'm withdrawing my invitation."

Jake smiled and shook his head, he admired candidness in women. "No Cassie, but I do have four children and I had to check with the babysitter."

"Oh, I see … and?"

"And she said she doesn't mind staying a few more hours."

Jake followed the little red car closely, his mind a maze of emotions. Considering the circumstances of their initial meeting, there was no way he would have even conceived the idea of asking her out. Yet here he was, on his way to her flat at *her* invitation. It seemed fate had given him a second chance with this lovely creature, he would have to be careful though, he must not move too quickly or else he may blow everything, and she didn't strike him as the type to give out too many opportunities freely.

Cassie threw a couple of steaks on the grill, a tossed green salad and found a bottle of red wine she had received as a Christmas present one year from someone whose name she couldn't recall. Their conversation had become stilted with Jake checking the time every five minutes or so. "That was a lovely meal, but I really should be going."

Everything had been going so well, yet during the last forty minutes the atmosphere could have been cut with a knife. She studied him carefully watching with great interest as he toyed with his glass. "Jake," he looked up, "Are you uncomfortable with me?"

He smiled and dropped his gaze back to his glass, "Is it that obvious?" She shrugged, "I'm sorry, it's just that I haven't been alone with a woman since my wife left two years ago, and it feels a little strange."

"Why? Are you practicing celibacy?" she asked with a hint of amusement.

It was a perfectly logical question; in fact he had been asked it many times by his mates over a beer. He had laughed and answered with either a rude gesture or a crude response, however, coming from her brought a tinge of scarlet to his cheeks, and he raised his glass and drained its contents concealing his embarrassment. He glanced at her over the rim; she was staring, waiting for his reply; finally, he lowered the glass "No of course not. It's just that when Rae, my ex wife left, Dane was 12, Jeffrey 5, Carly 3 and Felicity 2 and I didn't want to leave them while I went picking up women. I felt they needed my love more than I needed to make love, if you know what I mean."

Cassie nodded, she admired his principles, "Well I can understand that, but what I can't figure out, is why your wife didn't take them with her. I know I certainly would have."

"Well she does intend to, eventually. At the moment she is concentrating on establishing her career." It was a pitiful excuse, he knew it, and judging by the frown that instantly creased her brow, so did she. When she reached across and touched he cheek softly, he took her hand and kissed it lightly.

"It must have been very difficult for you, trying to cope with a separation, raise four children and work eight hours a day," she said softly.

Their hands remained comfortably entwined, he smiled, "I've been very lucky, I've got a great babysitter who has been very supportive, and I'm a market gardener, so when the need arose I simply worked after normal business hours, or left the majority of it to my two part time employees."

"Fortunate perhaps, but I still think you're marvelous."

His tender touch was arousing a stirring in her she hadn't felt for a long time. She knew he would be leaving soon, a thought which left a gaping hole in her heart. As though reading her mind, he glanced at his watch, "Well Cassie, I really must be going," his lips lingered on her hand, almost as though he was toying for time. They rose and moved towards the front door. Jake cupped her face with his hands and brushed his mouth softly over hers, the sweet aroma of her perfume teasing his senses, he was being drawn to her and the will to leave was rapidly dissipating. Her magnetic aura had captured his soul, his feet seemed cemented to the floor. They stared silently at each other for a moment, and then Jake pulled Cassie against him; she wrapped her arms around his neck and molded her body into his. His kiss was deep and urgent, denoting the years of abstinence. Cassie felt on fire, her heart was racing; she couldn't let him go, not now. When he finally relinquished her mouth, she gripped his hand like a vice and led him to the bedroom. There was no argument, no pleas towards rationality. He wanted her as much as she wanted him, and he was drowning in lust. He had gone too far, his body was screaming for the release it had been deprived of.

Jake watched as she removed her clothes revealing her nakedness. He felt as though he was witnessing the birth of a new blossom. Passion and sensuality vibrated between them, she inched slowly towards him with the grace of a swan. His own movements were jerky and awkward, he felt stupid, like an amateur. He fumbled and cursed when his zip caught on his under shorts and refused to move any further. Cassie laughed, "Here let me," she released it easily and he blushed.

They lay on the bed, their naked bodies melded in a slow rhythmic dance. She writhed and moaned with pleasure beneath his touch, until she felt his arousal pressing urgently between her thighs. She reached for him, guiding him smoothly until the depth of his penetration filled her completely. Their union was like a bolt of electricity, sparks surged through their bodies until both exploded in a shower of total climax.

Rae traced the soft bristles across her forehead. It was no use, she couldn't concentrate. Nothing was working and she was almost tempted to take up her Father's offer of a job. She placed the brush despondently back into its tray, removed her robe and climbed naked into bed. Lying back against the pillows she thought of Jake. There was so much bitterness in him. When she had fulfilled her promise to her Father and rung him, it had been exactly as she expected. He had told her to mind her own business. "Think of the children," she had argued.

"Don't speak to me about the children," he retaliated. "I'm not the one that deserted them, and as long as they are cared for properly, which they are, you have nothing to *bitch* about!" The receiver had promptly been slammed in her ear, leaving the tears to flow freely down her face. He was right, she should have taken them with her, but she needed time; time to find herself, time to grow as a person, not just somebody's wife or Mother. And now, now that she knew what she wanted out of life she didn't have the means to support them. But one day; one day that would change and she would have her children with her again. The phone rang bringing her from a blissful doze she had finally slipped into. "Hello."

"Mrs. Marshall, it's Skye Kennedy, I apologise for the late hour."

Rae stifled a yawn, "That's alright," and as complete consciousness encompassed her, she sat up rigid, her voice now gripped with fear, "What is it Skye? Is something wrong with one of the children?"

"No, it's nothing like that, but I do have a bit of a problem. I agreed to watch them until ten thirty, but it's already after eleven and I'm afraid I can't stay any longer."

Rae exhaled with relief as the image of the middle aged rotund woman on the other end of the receiver came to mind. In fact, she had actually interviewed Skye before she left, and it was her Motherly qualities that inspired Rae to hire her. That plus her reliability and promptness was another attribute that impressed both her and Jake, however, Skye also expected the same consideration, and if she agreed to a specified time, then that was the exact time she expected Jake to be home. "Well I'm sorry, but I don't really see how I can help you. Didn't he leave a number with you?"

"No he didn't and to be perfectly honest I'm a little peeved by his tardiness. Could you possibly come and relieve me, I *REALLY* must get home." Rae thought for a moment, but then as inconvenient as it was, what could she do? After all they were *HER* children too. "Of course, but give me thirty minutes at least."

Skye could be almost heard to smile, "Certainly, and thanks. I really am sorry to do this to you, but as I said I must get home, Roger barely sees me as it is."

Rae sighed, "Don't give it a second thought, I'm only sorry you were put out this way." The receiver fell into the cradle with an almighty crash. The room was engulfed with her fury, her blonde head shook frantically; *this* was outrageous. Without much consideration, she threw on an old pair of faded jeans and checked shirt, cursing Jake profusely as she flounced out the door.

Jake opened his eyes, Cassie was lying on his arm and it was going numb. He maneuvered it slowly from beneath her and glanced at his watch, 4:00a.m. "Shit!" His sleeping bed partner raised reluctant eyelids and yawned, "What's the matter?"

"I fell asleep, that's what, and I should have been home hours ago. Boy is Skye going to be pissed off, I'll catch you later." She watched him with amusement as he raced to the front door, his hasty attempt at stepping into his shoes failing miserably. After she heard him drive off, she snuggled back against the pillows and smiled happily; HE was the one. They had made love over and over for hours and each time had ended in waves of ecstasy, yes HE was definitely the one, she was sure of it.

Rae heard the key in the lock; she was seething with contempt by now, and sat from her laying position on the lounge ready for battle. As he walked into the room, she flew at him, "*Where the hell have you been*? Or should I say what gutter have you been sleeping in?"

He stared at her in surprise, but then he should have guessed Skye would contact her, his lowered in shame.

"Good Lord, you're not drunk, you're stone cold sober!"

He blushed and she covered a gasp with her hand, "Don't tell me; you've been with a woman haven't you? You left the kids until this ungodly hour, so you could screw the arse off some slut!" Her voice was foreboding. Jake was confused, he felt outraged at her tone, yet embarrassed at the truth. He wanted to scream at her in defense and yet apologize also. He opted for silence, his eyes averting hers. "Well Jake Marshall, next time you want to spend the night screwing; you can tell Skye not to *ring me*!" She grabbed her keys and flung her arm out as she passed, catching him hard in the chest, "*BASTARD*!"

Chapter 3

It was just before noon before Cassie dragged herself from the comfort of her bed; she showered and dressed in a simple cotton shift, her hair braided tightly to the back of her head. It was frightfully hot, yet the ambience in her small flat was magical, she felt no heat only the radiation from her body still emanating from her perfect night of love making. The sensation of his touch as he explored every part of her body with slow moving fingers and tongue still lingered and continued to send shivers down her spine.

She sat at her small dressing table and picked up a photo of a very pretty, petite redhead, smiling brightly at her; tracing her finger slowly around the woman's face, she smiled back. Dear Philyce, through her usual unreliability, she had inadvertently done her an enormous favor. A friend of many years, she had stuck by Cassie through her own divorce from Gavin and had even decided to come with her to Perth in her quest for a new beginning. Together they had hitched from Sydney, catching rides from the forever onset of semi trailers making the arduous journey across the long, awesome yet boring Nullarbor Plain. Between them, they had less than three hundred dollars, therefore, had to pay some of the truck drivers in kind; (which she now regrets deeply and has no

20

intention of telling ANYONE.) A few were older men with families, only too grateful for the company, but most were young guys, and only wanted money or the OTHER. Still Cassie had anticipated this and had come prepared. On the other hand, Philyce had been appalled, but then that was just Philyce, a simple, naïve, sweet country girl. The type men look for in wives not lovers. Philyce had managed to retain her virginity by pleading innocence and crying a lot. Cassie had paid for the both of them.

They had stayed at the YWCA until Cassie found a job selling shoes in a large department store, and Philyce a receptionist in a Solicitor's office. It was then that they moved into these flats, Cassie on the ground floor, her friend on the second. When Cassie eventually got fed up of commuting to the City by bus day after day, she had gone into debt buying her small red Cortina. As though in tune with her thoughts, her friend knocked on the unlocked door and walked in: "Hi, I'm sorry about last night, but you see the only reason I suggested the Valencia was because Don (her boss and also 'friend') said he was going that way, then, would you believe it, at the last minute changed his mind. I tried to ring, but you'd already left." She inhaled deeply then sighed; "Are you terribly mad?!"

Astounded by this woman's ability to literally prattle on in one breath brought Cassie doubled over in laughter. Philyce slightly bemused and unaware of the joke, smiled faintly, "Does that mean yes or no?" Cassies' starry eyes twinkled impishly, "Well I should be, shouldn't I, and in fact I was absolutely furious to begin with," she had to laugh again at her friend's solemn face; "But then I met someone!"

Piercing emerald eyes widened, as her delicate red mouth parted in delight, "Really! That's wonderful, tell me more!"

Trying to conceal her bubbly mood and be casual, she

pointed to the chair, "Alright, sit down, but I'm not telling you everything, some parts are too personal."

Phil grimaced in disappointment, "Oh pooh, I suppose it'll be all the good bits," she sighed, "Oh well, tell me anyway, I've a good imagination, I can piece the spicy bits together myself."

"Is that right, and to think all this time I thought you were completely chaste." They both laughed, Cassie sat opposite and related the story from the near miss meeting on the road, to their drinks at the hotel.

Phil's face wrinkled in disgust, "That's it; that's all! Really Cassie I certainly wouldn't classify that as earth shattering news.

With fingers knitted, Cassie stretched her arms above her head and yawned, "I told you I wasn't going to tell you everything. One thing I did forget, he's got four children."

The redhead flinched, "Ouch; that could cause a few headaches!"

"No, I don't think so, apart from the eldest who's 14, they're still pretty young." She lifted her hands to her head and began absently twisting her braid, "they should be reasonably opened minded about this, if anything eventuates between Jake and me that is, and I'm certain I'll be able to handle any problems," she stated confidently.

Pools of green watched in fascination as Cassies' long slender fingers worked methodically, twisting and turning until strands of raven hair were released from their confines. She smiled inwardly; this was long time habit of hers whenever she felt insecure or afraid. "Did you tell him about Gavin?"

"No and I don't intend to. After all, I have no ties with Gavin, and since he's three thousand miles away, I don't think it really necessary."

Philyce raised her eyebrows, secrets were no way to start a relationship, "I know it's none of my business, but I'm going to give you some advice anyway. Don't hold anything back, and please don't rush into anything like you did before. I'd hate to see you fall on your face again."

Her fingers ceased their movement, "What are you talking about, I CHOSE to leave Gavin." There was a flicker of contempt in her voice, and Philyce suddenly felt defensive.

"Come off it Cassie, you were married thirteen months. Everybody knew it was a mistake except you of course. No you had to rush into marriage at 18, after knowing him only three months. Then low and behold, suddenly you discover you're not compatible and race off, leaving the poor guy shattered wondering what he'd done wrong," she softened her tone, "All I'm trying to say Cass, is, please don't make the same mistake again. Do you know what I mean?"

Anger began in the pit of her stomach. What the hell did she know about it, SHE, who had never even been touched by a man, was trying to lecture on how to go about a relationship?

"Yes Philyce, I know what you mean, but you sure as hell don't. In the first place who said anything about getting married, and, in the second place I left Gavin because he couldn't give me children. He was infertile and no good to me. I only married him to have a baby, so what was the point in hanging around when that wasn't possible. IF or WHEN Jake and I ever discuss the possibility of marriage at least I know he can father …" She had been prattling on unaware of the silent change in her friend's face. Now that it was obvious, it was too late, she had said too much. Phil's eyes had darkened her mouth a tight line. Her mind was in turmoil. It was through her Cassie had met Gavin. He had been HER boyfriend, and she had loved him deeply, yet when she saw him literally drowning in Cassie's eyes the first time they met, she had stepped aside allowing what she believed to be true love prevail.

If she had known all those years ago her friend's real motive, she never would have let him go, not without a fight anyway. She felt betrayed and although Gavin was unaware of the depth of her feelings, Cassie was. She had confided in her, yes Cassie knew, yet she hadn't deterred his advances, in fact she had reveled in them, flirting with him at every available moment until finally they had slept together. Philyce had been terribly hurt, yet she had walked away like a true friend should. She had coveted Cassie and fought desperately her feeling of contempt; in fact it took all her strength to make herself forgive them, because she assumed they loved each other beyond reproach. And now; Cassie watched as Philyce rose slowly. She cursed mentally at revealing her secret to the one person she had vowed she wouldn't, "Phil I …,"

"You bitch! You fucking slut! How could you have done that to me? You knew how much I loved Gavin. I HATE you!!"

Pools of unshed tears clouded her eyes, she moved towards the door, and then turned to face Cassie again; "I never, ever want to speak to or lay eyes on you again. Furthermore, if I ever have the misfortune to cross your path, I shall pretend I don't know you, because Cassandra Nelson I DON'T! And should you happen to see me first, please do me the courtesy of doing the same." The door slammed and she was gone.

Cassie stared after her, then looked away, an inert smile crossed her face, she would be back; they'd had many fights over the years and she always came back.

Guilt was something Cassie rarely suffered from. She was a user, always had been. She used her best friend to get to Gavin, and with her main objective in life being the need to have children, she had used him to accomplish this desire. After all, he was tall and handsome, a top football player, with eyes that could melt steel. Yes indeed, he was the perfect choice to sire her babies; unfortunately, virility didn't necessarily mean fertility, so now there was Jake. In no way did he fit into

Gavin's league, but, he was nice to look at, had reasonably strong features and was good in bed, but most importantly, he had already proved his fertility, so now she would use Jake.

As the months passed, Cassie made no effort to contact Philyce, who also remained obscure, but when she learned from Mr. Tyson, Phil had moved, with strict instructions not to reveal her new address; she experienced for the first time in many years, the slightest prick in her conscience.

Jake was completely overcome by her mystical magnetism, he was certain he felt more for her than she for him, but he didn't care, he had to have her no matter what. Cassie knew she had him in her power, she knew a marriage proposal was imminent, and when it happened she accepted without hesitation. The only thing that Jake was a little concerned about was the fact that to date she hadn't wanted to meet his children, and always had an excuse whenever he suggested it. But he had let it go, she had her reasons and one day she would open up and accept his kids and they would become a happy family with a loving Mother again. But for now he would let it ride and pushed his thoughts to the back of his mind.

He pulled her against him and squeezed her tenderly, "You've made me the happiest man in the world, and I promise I'll make you happy for the rest of your life. She combed her fingers through his hair and smiled casually, yes he would, at least until she got her children. The only obstacle was Jake's children; she hadn't met them but she knew they already didn't like the idea of their Father with another woman as he had told her of a conversation he'd had with them.

"Why do we have to have a Stepmother, we've got Mum," Dane had pouted.

"I'm aware of that, but your Mother doesn't live here anymore, and I think it would be nice to have a woman around to look after us."

Jeffrey seven, continued the argument, "Why can't you and Skye keep looking after us?"

Jake was extremely tired, he sighed, "Because I have to go to work mate, and since the garden is expanding," he paused, how could he make his explanation sound simple, "The plain truth is, I don't like leaving you with Skye all the time. After all she has got other things to attend to."

Carly, five, entered the conversation, "But daddy, we like Skye, why can't you marry her?" He looked at his small daughter and smiled at her innocence, "Because sweetheart, she is already married to Roger, remember." Her small impish face wrinkled in confusion; after all, if her Mother and Father were married once, yet her Father is going to marry someone else now, couldn't Skye do that as well?

"I don't see the problem Dad," Dane interrupted, trying to sound worldly and wise, "Skye loves us; she won't mind looking after us longer during the day." The inability to reason with his kids was trying his patience. "Dane, Cassie will love you also, and damn it I need a wife, can't you understand that?" He had to refrain from saying, "You're a big boy now, not a baby, and I have the same normal needs any man has." His eldest son read his mind, "Why can't you just go to a whore house when you need a woman?"

"What's a whore house Dad?" Jeffrey asked innocently.

"Nothing honey, just the name of a shop." He turned to Dane horrified by the candidness of his eldest son, his patience had run out. "How the hell do you know about such things," he roared.

Dane lowered his eyes, "I see movies and read books, and I'm not an infant Dad." Jake was stunned; whatever happened to Treasure Island and Swiss Family Robinson, he felt the heat rise in his cheeks, the knuckles on his clenched fist had turned white, he slammed it down heavily on the table. "I'm marrying

Cassie, and that's the end of it. She's coming here on Saturday to meet all of you, and by cripes you all will be nice … or else!!" They flinched at his thunderous voice, while the crockery shook precariously on the table from his demonstrative action. One by one they left, filing defiantly into their bedrooms, the youngest, Felicity, four, cradling and comforting her headless doll Betsy from behind.

It was the first weekend of August; Cassie sat nervously waiting for Jake. Her choice of dress, a grey pleated skirt and high frill necked blouse, was drab, too drab, and her hair pulled to the top of her head in a plaited knot, gave the appearance of an old school teacher. However, she had concluded she needed to appear Motherly rather than young and modern. Even Jake, when he arrived scowled at her appearance but said nothing.

The drive to Wanneroo was particularly pleasant. The heavy winter rains had left gardens verdant and fresh, and with the onset of spring only weeks away, the flowers were starting to point their delicate petals towards the warming sun. Cassie found her nervousness dissipating as she viewed the surroundings, allowing instead the sweet feeling of contentment wash over her.

Jake pulled into the drive of his modest three bedrooms home and she was aptly impressed. The foliage was as lush and lovely as those they had passed. The red brick house was surrounded by acres of vegetables growing proudly in the rich red earth. Pine trees tiered along the drive, while a covered pergola in front of the oriel, which she guessed was the living room, was adorned with several varieties of ferns. Cassie noticed the curtain move slightly, they were obviously being surveyed and once again the knots in her stomach began to tighten. He held her hand tightly as they approached the door, she felt secure beneath his grasp, but nevertheless as he turned the key, she instinctively retreated from his side. "What's the matter?" his asked feeling concern.

She faltered at the threshold, "I'm not so sure this is such a good idea. Maybe it's too soon to meet your kids."

Once again Jake reached for her hand, which she accepted gratefully, "Don't be silly darling, they're only children, not a lynching party." She flashed a hesitant smile, he was right; she was being ridiculous, after, all, what normal adult would be scared of four innocent children. Once inside, she automatically glanced in the sunken living/dining room on her right, towards the large bay window. No one was there.

He led her along the corridor then right into a modest but sufficient country kitchen, which also had access into the living area. Once again she found her eyes roaming to the large window; the curtain moved again and she drew in her breath in a startled gasp. Jake chuckled softly, "Don't worry; we don't have ghosts, only Dusty." At the mention of his name, an old collie hobbled from beneath the window into the kitchen. For the second time within minutes, she felt ridiculous and embarrassed. How could she have not noticed a dog that size lying there. The elderly culprit licked Jake's hand, and then returned to his cosy position. Grabbing her slim shoulders, he walked her to the table, where he pushed her gently into a chair, "Lighten up babe, anyone would think I was leading you to the gallows."

"Believe it or not, that's exactly how I feel," she tried to smile, but her mouth didn't want to co-operate. An old wood stove in the corner caught her attention temporarily taking her mind from the subject at hand, "What's with that? I thought that type of cooking went out with the Ark?"

He looked around, "What? Oh that. That was Rae's idea; she firmly believed the best cooks worked their culinary art over a combustion stove. When she left the first thing I did was buy a gas cooker."

The sound of children screeching merrily drifted in through the open kitchen window. She rose and peered out. Standing behind her, Jake wrapped his arms around her slim waist, drawing her against his masculine strength. Four children, all blondes, frolicked happily, while a rather round woman stood patiently hanging out what appeared to be a mountain of laundry. He kissed her cheek, "See just your average kids, no guns, knives or any other fatal instrument, and the lady up to her neck in laundry is my babysitter or for a better term lifesaver, is Skye. Are you ready to meet them now?"

Cassie licked her lips, the trace of amusement in his voice held no reassurance, "What if they don't like me Jake?" Turning her in his arms, he tilted her chin slightly and kissed her tenderly on the mouth. "Will you stop worrying; of course they'll like you." And after kissing her once more, slowly released the braid allowing the silky stands of hair frame her oval face. "How could they not like an angel?" A tinge of pink crept into her cheeks, this was the first time she had been referred to in that manner, and it was rather nice. Jake turned back to the window and called. One by one they looked towards him, and reluctantly made a move for the house. Now lined before her, Jake began the introductions. Scanning them briefly, Cassie noticed shades of mistrust and apprehension written all over their faces. But then how could she blame them. She was the first woman their Father had been with since their Mother left, a sudden wave of empathy washed over her.

With every name, he touched each on the head roughing their hair playfully, as though in reassurance. Cassie had to wonder as four pairs of pale green eyes gazed at her with frosty interrogation, who he was actually trying to reassure. Her voice wavered; even the youngest was looking at her with nothing short of contempt. Forcing a smile, she held out her hand to Dane, "How do you do."

Ignoring her hand is simply replied "Fine thanks."

His response held malice and Cassie suddenly felt very cold, it was obvious he had already formed an opinion. Again she offered her hand to Jeffrey, "And how are you?" The small boy stared, but offered no reply, she felt her brow grow wet with perspiration.

Carly placed her tiny hand in hers, then withdrew it as though it was on fire. Felicity's eyes hadn't left Cassie for a second. This giant lady was really scared, she could tell. Cassie came down to her level, "my; isn't that a pretty doll. What's her name?"

Her small voice whispered, "Betsy."

"What a lovely name. May I have a look?" At least this child was speaking to her, maybe if she gained her confidence the others would follow. Any illusions of that were dispersed when the doll was rapidly drawn closer to the little girls' chest.

"No! She doesn't like new people, they frighten her."

Cassie was shattered, and returned to her full height before any of them noticed the glassy redness occurring in her eyes, "Well I certainly wouldn't want that to happen." An awkward moment of silence had lapsed, before Cassie became aware someone was tugging at her skirt frantically. She looked down into Carly's fiery face, the stubborn rebellious line around the child's small mouth indicated she was about to be told off.

"Daddy says you're going to be our Mother, but I think you should know, we already have Mummy, and don't need a new one." Cassie glanced at Jake, a deep frown now across his brow. Obviously this wasn't going the way he had planned and he was not at all pleased.

"Actually Carly, I have no intention of replacing your Mother, no-one could do that unless you wanted them to, but

I am going to become your Stepmother, which simply means, I hope to be your friend and look after you, just like your real mummy would if she was here."

Jake silently applauded, he couldn't have put that any better himself, and the slight but definite smile on his daughter's tiny pink mouth was surely a sign of acceptance.

Skye had entered the room, and had been listening to the conversation unnoticed. When Jake directed the children into the bedroom, she approached Cassie. "Don't let them worry you too much dear, they are frightened of change. It took me several months before they finally realized I wasn't a monster with two heads. They'll accept you; just give them a little time."

"You think so? It seems to me they have already decided they hate me."

"You've already scored one point with Carly. They'll come around, you'll see." Extending her hand in welcome, she smiled, "By the way I'm Skyla, but everyone calls me Skye. I'm the babysitter when you need one, and as Jake says part of the furniture."

Cassie accepted the gesture. "I'm Cassandra Nelson, Cassie to my friends." And this warm sensitive woman was going to be just that, a friend and an ally, she could sense it. Perhaps even, the only one she would be able to turn to in the struggling months ahead.

Four impish faces stared at their Father. He was furious. For the last minute he had said nothing, just stood before them, hands on his head, staring at each one. They all jumped, when he threw his hands in the air and began to bellow, "That was the most appalling display of rudeness I have ever encountered in my life. And to think it came from MY children. I am SO disgusted I don't know whether to tan all your hides or simply pretend I don't know you!"

31

Dane sighed, "We don't like her."

Jake grabbed the boy's shoulders, shaking him roughly, "You don't even know her; how can you possibly judge so quickly!"

They stood in silence, a pact had been formed, no strange woman was going to web her way around their Father and into their lives. No sir, no way. Jake released Dane and walked to the door, but before leaving warned, "If that EVER happens again, you will ALL feel my wrath, like you've never felt before. And, as for now, you can stay in here until you decide to be more civil!" He slammed the door knowing they had chosen to be difficult and would probably stay in the room all day, rather than give in: Which they did.

Chapter 4

Rae approached her Father in his office early the next morning. "Dad, can you spare five minutes, I need to talk to you." Carl pushed his chair back, crossed his legs over the corner of the desk and knotted his fingers behind his head.

"Sure honey, sit down. It's Sunday, remember; nobody breaks the law on a Sunday because they are all too busy sleeping off their hangover," he stated sarcastically.

She slid gracefully into the well worn leather chair, "I had a phone call from Dane last evening. It seems Jake is planning to re-marry." The intimate pleasure this news gave could not be hidden, he beamed broadly, *and finally* Rae would be completely rid of this parasite. "That's great honey, now we can *ALL* stop worrying." The hazel eyes that had taken on a green tinge, matching her pale green slack suit widened; her voice trembled slightly.

"That's the problem Dad, *I AM* concerned." Carl's heart raced, surely she wasn't contemplating thwarting Jake's marital intentions in order to re-kindle their pathetic relationship, because, if so he would throttle her himself.

Rae continued, "Apparently Jake brought this woman home to meet the kids yesterday, and Dane claims she insisted they be sent to their room. He doesn't know why, but anyway, it seems they were locked in there all day without any meals, only to be released when Jake drove what's her name home," she waved her hand dismissing Cassie's name casually.

Carl's stomach rolled as he laughed with relief, "You make it sound as though they were imprisoned." Obviously she wasn't impressed by his reaction, the somber set of her jaw implied the seriousness of the matter; Carl rolled his eyes, "Surely you don't actually believe that crap?"

Rae lifted her small shoulders, "I don't know Dad, I can't imagine Jake doing something like that for anybody, but Dane was so upset it got me wondering." Her long fingers twisted a handkerchief nervously; he removed his legs from the mahogany desk and sat erect. "Listen honey, teenagers have an active imagination and a tendency to tell outright lies, as you well know. I mean you used to tell some whoppers when you were a kid." Whenever Rae couldn't get her Father to take her seriously, she would cradle her face with her hands and stifle a sob. He would sigh and begin to strum whatever was in front of him with his fingers. She heard the familiar tapping on the desk and knew it had worked, again.

Carl pursed his lips, this sounded like something out of a classic child abuse case. Next she would be telling him how they were beaten until they were black and blue, in which case he would surely scream. As much as he disliked Jake he had always been a kind and patient Father. In fact, in all the years he had known him, he had only ever heard him raise his voice to those kids twice, and, with her own admission, Rae was always the punisher, not Jake. "I'm sorry, but I'm just not buying it! Perhaps you should ask Jake yourself."

"Well, I suggested that, but Dane burst into tears and begged me not to. He claims Jake had threatened to beat them within an inch of their life if he mentioned it to anyone, especially me."

Carl stared at his daughter with disbelief, how could she be so gullible or is she just plain and simply stupid? He let out a very deep sigh, "Rae, darling, you were married to Jake for how long … you of all people saw his good side and his bad. Now given the facts, can you actually believe any of this trash that is coming out of your sons' mouth, I mean seriously Rae you know that man better than anyone. However, if you DO believe that garbage just take the kids away from there to live with you."

Rae crossed her well formed legs, and toyed uncomfortably with her purse, her eyes concentrating on anything other than her Father's stern face. She sighed heavily; "Dad my career is finally starting to take off. Over the last few months I've managed to complete two paintings, and I actually have a dealer interested in my work. He has commissioned me to paint three more Landscapes and two Seascapes, after which he plans to have a showing. It could be months before I can do anything concrete with the children. Do you suppose you and Mum could take them?" She finally met his gaze, "I mean only temporary of course. It would be just until I get on my feet?" Throughout her spiel, he had practically mimed word for word, it was the exact crap she had given him two weeks ago or was it a month?

He studied her anxious eyes carefully; dark shadows indicated she hadn't slept much. Understanding his daughter was somewhat enigmatic. Her obvious concern was sincere enough, yet, she still placed her as yet unsuccessful career before the welfare of her children. Slowly he shook his head, more in wonder than refusal "You know your Mother and I would love to take them, but you're forgetting one thing: Jake. How do you think he'd react if I casually rolled up there and informed him I was taking his kids off him, especially since I'm not supposed to know anything? What reason could I give? My daughter doesn't trust your new wife to be so she's asked me to take over the responsibility of the children until she lands on her feet?"

Rae's hopeful look turned to despair. When she wiped away a tear Carl instantly regretted the cruelty and sarcasm of his words. He moved from behind his desk to side and lightly placed a hand on her shoulder. "I tell you what I will do though; how about if I call in and see my grandchildren one day this week, and check it out for myself. Because I have to say truthfully darling, I think Dane is telling one big whopper!"

The return of hope in her watery eyes appeased his guilt; she smiled warmly, yet spoke with consternation, "That would be wonderful Dad, but you will be tactful won't you?"

A single strand of silken hair stood proudly erect atop her golden head, he smoothed it down lovingly, "Of course."

Carl waited until Wednesday afternoon when he knew the boys would be home from school. Skye greeted him graciously, Sergeant Barrett, how nice to see you, please come in."

"*Grandpa*!" He had barely crossed the threshold as the name echoed around the room. One by one they torpedoed into his arms, almost knocking him down. "Wow, that's the sort of greeting I like," he laughed, stroking each individual head.

"Did you bring us anything Grandpa?" He gazed down at Carly, her delicate faced framed with golden curls, while large green eyes sparkled with excitement. Carl placed his thumb across her tiny pink mouth which was slightly open in a broad smile. How his little namesake reminded him of his own precious daughter.

"But of course my darling" he replied reaching into his pocket and extracting a large bag of caramel sweets, "Now make sure you share them honey, *BUT* ... not until *AFTER* dinner mind!"

Grabbing the sweets, she skipped happily into her room, with Felicity hot on her heels, demanding to see what Grandpa had bought.

Dane stood before him, 'my goodness he was getting tall' he thought as he threw a lazy arm around the lad's shoulder, "So how have you been?"

"Great, I got an A in maths; want to see my report?!" His chest was puffed out in pride; Carl smiled, Rae used to do the same thing when she received good marks at school. "Sure!"

Dane raced off leaving Jeffrey, "And what about you half pint, how's life been treating you?"

The boy shrugged, then his face lit up in, "The tooth fairy came last night and left me *two dollars*!" He opened his mouth exposing a large gap with a tooth has once been. Carl combed his fingers through the young boy's hair. Normally anyone doing that was regarded as 'the pits', however his Grandfather was different, after all he was a detective. He caught bad people and put them in jail, which made him somewhat of a hero in the small boys' eyes. "Gosh Jeff, if you lose any more teeth, you'll soon be rich at that rate." At that moment Skye entered the room carrying a tray of steaming coffee. Jeffrey raced off mentally calculating how much he would have if he lost his remaining teeth in a hurry.

"How's Jake these days Skyla (he was the only one that called her by her given name on the odd occasion); behaving himself?"

"Oh yes, it's marvelous the change in him since he met Cassie," biting her bottom lip, she placed the tray on the glass table. Should she have mentioned Cassie, after all it was not her place to gossip about Jake's private affairs.

Carl sensed her discomfort, "It's alright Skyla, I think it's wonderful if Jake has met somebody else. What is she like?"

Her small black eyes averted his, while she avoided

answering his question. Even though Carl had previously considered his grandchildren look far from abused, her evasion left him wondering if perhaps there was in fact some foundation in Dane's story, and was about to question it out right, when she responded, "Please don't think I'm rude Sergeant Barrett, but I really don't think it's my place to discuss the matter."

Carl rubbed his chin, of course, how foolish of him. Skye's reluctance was obviously due to Rae. "I don't wish to appear nosy Skye, but if you're concerned about my daughter, don't be. Rae already knows Jake is planning to get married; Dane phoned her the other evening.

That was just what the middle aged woman needed to hear, she smiled, now only too pleased to talk about it. "Well, to tell you the truth, I only met her briefly on Saturday, but she seemed very nice, and I know Jake is completely smitten by her." Her smile faded into a disapproving scowl, "Unfortunately, the children aren't quite so keen to have another woman around the house. I witnessed a dreadful scene; they couldn't have been ruder to Miss Nelson if they'd tried. Jake was furious, he told them to stay in their room until they could be polite to her. And do you know those little devils opted to stay in their room, rather than extend a little friendship." Her graying head shook slightly, she sighed, "They even refused to come out and eat with her."

Carl had taken a seat, listening intently. One thing he knew he was good at, and that was detecting unsaid words and lies. For all intense purposes, this woman was speaking honestly. With one arm folded across his chest, he propped the other under his chin. "What did Jake do about that?"

"Well, he did the same thing I would have done; he told them they could jolly well go without. That poor woman was so upset, she asked Jake to take her home immediately." A broad grin had broken her staid face, "Mind you, missing lunch certainly made a difference at dinner time. Those little terrors almost cleaned the design off their plates."

"I see," Carl locked his hands behind his head, "And they stayed in their room until dinner time, did you say?"

Skye frowned, this was starting to sound like an interrogation, "Heavens no, they were only in there until Cassie left, and as I said, she went straight away. No they weren't in there very long at all."

It was a well known fact, Dane had an over active imagination, and to be blatantly honest, a born liar, but this little stretch of the truth was a bloody whopper. At that exact moment Carl felt like taking the boy across his knee and *REALLY* beating him within an inch of his life. He drank his coffee slowly, waiting for the elusive boy to return. After twenty minutes, Dane still hadn't surfaced. Carl surmised he had overheard the conversation with Skye, and, realizing his Mother had mentioned the ordeal to him, was astute enough to keep from sight. He considered confronting him about it, but decided that may make matters more complicated. Instead, he returned the cup to the tray, stood and stretched, "Well Skyla, Dane was going to bring me his report card, but it appears he has been side tracked, and, I really must get back to work. I'll sneak out so they don't make a fuss. Say goodbye for me, and tell Jake I'll ring him sometime." He wouldn't, he knew he wouldn't, so did Skye and no doubt Jake, but what the hell, he had to say something of that nature. She nodded silently and led him to the door.

Dane sat on the edge of his bed, the crumpled report on his lap. He had heard the conversation alright and was furious. It certainly hadn't occurred to him his Mother would tattle to her Father, but it was clear she had, and obviously this little visit was of an official capacity. Boy, how stupid could he have been, thinking she would keep it all under her hat. He had thought, or rather hoped, his tall tale would bring her sympathetically to their side. She was supposed to tell them not to worry, and that she was going to take them home to live with her. But, it had back fired and unless he could think of another way, they would have to endure life with that raven haired witch. Tilting his head back, he smiled sardonically; *Like hell!*"

Chapter 5

Cassie decided against confronting the kids again, at least for a while, so declined Jake's request to spend Christmas Day with them.

They ate in silence; Jake threw a glance towards his oldest son, who was toying with his food. The traditional turkey had been replaced by roast chicken, and Dane considered this on a par with toast on Easter Sunday instead of hot cross buns. Jake rose and took his empty plate to the sink, he gazed silently through the window at a small bird flitting happily in his favorite wattle tree, the delicate yellow blossoms seemed to dance romantically under its' weight. Some Christmas this was; the woman he loved was spending it alone, he had forgotten to buy the blessed turkey, none of them were overly impressed with their gifts, and now Dane sat there looking as though it was his last supper. Instead of being filled with joy, he felt completely depressed. Without turning, he spoke softly, his words deliberately slow, "We're getting married on March 3rd."

The silence screamed up at him, he could feel Dane's eyes boring into his skull. A chair scraping across the vinyl indicated someone was leaving the room. When he finally faced them, Jeffrey was absent. Surprise or even complete shock he expected; what he saw wasn't. Dane's face, a heavily lined ashen mask, seemed to have aged seventy years, while the two girls stared blindly, as though in a coma. Grayness encompassed the room; he pivoted his focus back to his conversation, "I haven't just announced the end of the world, you know!"

The lad's mouth moved, yet it took a few seconds before anything was audible, "But I thought."

Their eyes locked, "You thought what!?"

Dane shrugged, "You thought that because Cassie hasn't been back since that outrageous display you and the others put on, I wasn't seeing her anymore!" It was difficult swallowing the lump in his throat, tears were biting, threatening, but he wouldn't let his Father see him cry. "I knew you were still seeing her, I just didn't think she would marry you after …"

Fury surged through Jake's veins; adrenalin pumped his blood at a frightening rate, "After your disgusting attempt to thwart her. Fortunately for you Dane, Cassie understood your motives; otherwise, you *STILL* wouldn't be able to sit down. It was her idea to keep away, to give you all time to adjust to the idea." Dane wiped his eyes with the back of his hand; right now he felt very small and insignificant. His Father was going to marry her, they would have babies and before long, he and his siblings would be pushed to the back like old stock. Carly and Felicity looked towards their brother, who was trying unsuccessfully not to cry. The youngest child really didn't care all that much what happened. All she knew was that Dane had said Cassie was bad, and if she moved in with them, they would probably be sent to a foster home, whatever that was. Yet somehow, she knew in her small heart, her Father would not let that happen, and certainly wouldn't be with someone that was bad.

Jake strode to the boy's bedroom and literally hauled Jeffrey back by the ear. The announcement his Father had made was tearing at his heart, he too, had been told the onset of a stepmother meant without doubt, foster homes for them. And now, all he could imagine was life somewhere else, with someone else. It was unthinkable. His stinging ear was released, replaced by a sudden shove in the back towards his vacant chair, "*Sit!*"

Frustration absorbed every pore, Jake threw his arms in the air, turbulent eyes followed in a prayer gesture; "Just what *IS* the problem? If Cassie resembled Medusa, I just might, *MIGHT*, be able to understand your disapproval, but … she's a wonderful caring human being. You couldn't ask for a kinder person to care for you." The silence was deafening, they were all staring at Dane, he was the spokesman, and he had to answer. Finally, he raised his tear stained face towards his Father, "*WE DON'T LIKE HER!*"

Jake sighed, his voice deep and menacing enveloped the room, "You mean, *YOU* don't like her, and somehow you've managed to coerce the others with your opinion." Three bowed heads didn't budge, whilst Dane held his Father's gaze with contempt, "I'm going to marry Cassie whether any of you like it or not. If you don't wish to be there, that's fine, but either way, there *WILL BE* a wedding; and nobody is going to ruin that day for me. Do you understand!?" There was no room for argument, one by one they alighted and filed silently into their rooms.

Somehow Cassie allowed herself to be coerced into spending New Year with them; however she refused his offer to pick her up. If she was going to be thrown into the lions' den, at least she was going to have her own means of escape. The hazy dimness of dusk enclosed around her as she had been driving painfully slow towards the 'fire pit'. Tight knots gripped her stomach when she pulled into the drive-way. This was going to be one hell of an ordeal, especially if it was going to be a replica of her first encounter. Oh well, at least Skye would be here tonight, and hopefully, she would be able to draw strength from the older woman's wisdom.

Jake heard her car and gave the four a fleeting look of warning before opening the door. They glanced at her briefly as she entered; only Carly offered some form of welcome with very slight but still distinct smile. Cassie felt a glimmer of hope however slight it may have been, at least it was there, and, with a bit of luck, possibly a friendship may evolve. Jake stormed to the television, switching off the program they were watching; Dane glared with protest.

"Don't you have something to say to Cassie?" Defiant lines creased his face, and judging by the reaction of the others, they were waiting for him to speak first. A sudden occurrence flashed through her mind, it was he who had the power of acceptance within his grasp. For reasons he only knew, Dane seemed to have melded their minds with his own. Regardless of their Father, they were frightened to like her in case if offended their older brother. His wrath was worse than Jakes'. Anyone who maintained that much control and esteem, must be respected, for the holder of that much influence, no matter how misguided, would one day go far.

On the other hand, Jake did not agree. With eyes almost black from rage, his fist poised, made a move for the boy. Cassie reached out and grabbed his arm, "No Jake; please don't make a fuss." She ran her fingers gently down his cheek, "I know he is being rude, but punishing him on my account will only make it worse." Dane could be seen from the corner of her eye, staring in disbelief and mistrust. As though to remind him, she added, "He's only a boy yet Jake, give him time."

A boy! Rage was building tempestuously within; that performance may have fooled his Father, but it certainly didn't fool him.

Further discussion ceased as Skye and her husband Roger, appeared at the open door. The night dragged endlessly on; Cassie felt as though she was sitting on a time bomb; even moving outside beneath the starry sky, and the warm gentle breeze caressing her damp brow could not relax her. She was an outcast, a leper, and should not have come despite Jake's objections.

Skye and Jake tried to include her in their conversations, however, for some reason Rae's name kept cropping up, if not by them, then by the children who had managed to monopolize the adults' attention most of the night. By the time midnight finally arrived, she'd had enough. Jake pulled her gently from her chair, "Happy New Year darling," and cupping her face with his hands kissed her tenderly, his tongue seeking hers. Sparks of electricity shot through her body, but no matter how excited his touch left her, she was definitely not staying the night. He released her mouth slowly, his hands still held her face, "It's been dreadful for you, hasn't it?" Their eyes fused, he would never know just how dreadful. She made a move to speak, then covered his hands with hers and brought them to his side. Panic stabbed at his heart, her face was blank, void of emotion, he had the distinct feeling she was about to turn and flee from his life forever, until he felt small hands grasping his torso. Obviously she had seen them coming over his shoulder, and retracted, allowing them access. Before she turned towards Skye, he imagined he saw tears in her eyes. His heart went out to her, and instead of kissing his four children frolicking around him, at that moment he wished they hadn't been born.

Dane was approaching, for an instant Cassie thought he was making his way towards her, until she realized it was Skye's arms he sought. He glared at her, his mouth mocking, slithers of hatred glistened under the moonlight mirroring his thoughts. There was no mistaking that look; she knew without doubt what his New Year resolution was.

For a whole second Cassie wanted to run; run as fast as she could away from this family; until she looked at Jake. His eyes said it all. His love for her could not be denied and his disappointment in his children was breaking his heart. She stood and gazed at the stars, and almost as though the wind whispered to her, at that precise moment she knew, she could not leave him. *HE* was the one and he needed her now more than ever. If she was to go and forfeit a life with a man she adores for the sake of four ungrateful children, she would be a fool, they would have won. No it wasn't going to happen. Not only was she going to stay the night with Jake, they were getting married on March 3rd and if the brats didn't want to come; that was fine with her.

Chapter 6

Quitting her job was easy; moving in with them two weeks prior to the wedding was not. Dane leaned propped against the entry wall, while she and Jake unloaded the car. Meticulously they worked, bringing in her luggage and personal effects, unpacking, and placing her items carefully in the wardrobe, all the while his bewitching eyes followed their every move, his silent stance speaking volumes. Cassie felt she was under a microscope, his presence unnerved her, but as that was his intention, she went about her business trying to ignore him.

Jake brought the last case in. He had watched his son silently for the last thirty minutes. The atmosphere was thick and like ice, the boys' face held no sign of emotion, just a blank mask of nothing. Finally Jake sighed and turned to the boy, "What are you doing son?"

He shrugged, "Nothing."

"Well then if you have no intention of helping, can you do nothing somewhere else? This house is small enough without having to maneuver around you."

A captured look of pain and denial spread swiftly over his face, "Sure Dad, I know when I'm not wanted." He turned and walked towards the back door, Jake called after him, but it was too late, he had already disappeared from view. Jake punched the door frame and sighed; "*Damn!*"

Cassie stepped towards him and put her arms around his neck, "Don't worry about it Jake, he's being deliberately difficult to punish you for bringing me here."

This was the first negative thing she had said, and it took him by surprise, yet it made sense. After all he had asked all his children at one time or another, to leave the room for whatever reason, without any offense being taken. He lifted her hand to his lips and kissed her long slender fingers tenderly. The lingering fragrance of her perfume wafted up from her wrists, tantalizing his senses. How he wanted to pull her against his body, and make love right then and there, but the children were out playing in the yard and could come in at any moment. "You're right, I guess he's going to play these games until he accepts us being married, or make life miserable for everyone until he's old enough to move out."

Tiny lines appeared in the corners of her almond shaped eyes as she smiled, "Don't blame him Jake, his security is threatened, and until he realizes nothing is going to change, he is going to test us both. I'll make something tempting for dinner, maybe that will soften his mood."

Cassie spent the afternoon in the kitchen. When she called them for dinner, the kitchen table was adorned with steaming roast beef, baked potatoes green beans and pea soup. Jake held his stomach and inhaled deeply, "My goodness, the aroma in this room is simply sensational."

Jake sat at the head of the table; Cassie sat beside him on his right. Jeffrey stood beside her and in a very small voice complained, "That's where I sit."

His Father shot him a warning look, but Cassie help up her hand, "I'm so sorry Jeffrey, and I should have realized you all have your special place at the table." She stood waiting until all were seated and took the chair opposite Jake, only to have Carly inform "That's where Mum used to sit." Cassie wasn't sure whether this little bit of trivia was meant to encourage or discourage her and looked over at Jake for help.

"That's right sweetheart, and since Cassie is going to be your Stepmother, I guess that means that is her chair now." This explanation was accepted and the small girl smiled and nodded her head.

They plodded through the meal silently, Jeffrey scoffed it down, but Dane did little more than push his food around the plate. The girls managed the soup but were too full to complete the main course. Jake turned to Dane "What's the matter son; you haven't touched your food?"

"Guess I'm not hungry, can I be excused."

"Why don't you have the soup at least, it's delicious?"

"I don't like pea soup," he glanced sideways towards Cassie. She stood and began clearing the table.

"What's for dessert?" Jeffrey asked.

"Oh gosh, I'm so sorry; I didn't have time to make any." The truth was she simply wasn't accustomed to having dessert and hadn't even given it a thought but made a mental note for next time.

"Gee Dad, Mum and Skye always made dessert," he stated ignoring her apology. "Cassie just said she didn't have time to prepare anything; I'm sure she'll try and make you something tomorrow."

She stood at the sink, her back to them, listening to Jake patronize the boy with as much patience as he could muster. Trying to follow her advice and give them time was becoming increasingly difficult, especially since they appeared to be making no effort whatsoever. In fact, if it wasn't for her desire to have a baby and reluctance to play the dating game again, she would pack her bags and walk out the door right now. She really loved Jake but this was all becoming way too difficult and just didn't seem worth it.

Later that night she lay in bed gazing through the window watching the stars; wondering if perhaps she should move out and find somewhere to rent until the children have a better understanding of the situation. They could postpone the wedding that would be no problem; and maybe just maybe the children may come to accept her after she's been in their lives a bit longer. At that moment Jake emerged from the bathroom, a towel hugging his hips tightly. Lowering himself beside her, he kissed the tip of her nose, "It's been a lousy day for you, I'm so sorry."

Placing a finger over his mouth she whispered, "I hope you don't intend to spend the rest of your life apologizing when things don't go right for me."

He brushed her cheek gently with his hand, "Only if my kids are the cause." He slid the fine straps of her nightgown down revealing her breasts, however instead of the usual tingling this action normally caused, she suddenly felt very weary. Somehow making love with his children sleeping on either side of the bedroom disconcerted her. She felt very small and insecure at this moment and even the warmth of his strong arms around her could not break her mood. "Jake, it's been an extremely long toilsome day; all I want to do right now is nestle against you and fall asleep in your arms.

Jake feathered his fingers along the contour of her semi naked body; he wanted her so much he was on fire. Her raven hair released from the usual chignon shrouded the pillow like a halo, her full breasts moved rhythmically in time with her slow breathing; he couldn't stand it. How could she expect him to lay beside her, feeling her warm breath kiss his neck, and not make love to her? "Cassie please you're torturing me." He gazed into her motionless face; she was fast asleep. Very softly he kissed her soft parted mouth and pulled the sheet across her body.

The next ten days were a myriad of confusion. Jake's idyll of family life was rapidly turning into a horror story. He could see what was happening, but was powerless to stop it. Dane was not eating and had dropped at least nine pounds in weight. When Jeffrey was not comparing everything Cassie did to Rae, the girls were. Carly was having a recurring nightmare of being abandoned, waking in a bath of perspiration and screaming for her Mother to come back, but it was Cassie that worried him the most. She had withdrawn into another dimension and had even considered postponing the wedding which he absolutely refused to do. She rarely spoke and moved around the house as though in a trance. Even their sex had become mechanical. The warm vibrant woman of a few weeks ago had gone, instead, he felt as though he was making love to a robot. She'd just lay there until he'd finished, then turn to the window and stare into the night.

Jake locked up and turned the lights off. The children had gone to bed just after eight, Cassie had retired soon after. He entered the bedroom quietly, expecting her to be asleep; instead she sat on the edge of the bed gazing fixedly through the window. The full moon emitted an eerie light around the room; with deliberate slowness he undressed, then slid across the bed placing his hand on her smooth naked back. She bowed her head at his touch, speaking softly, her voice flat, vacant of emotion, "They don't want me here Jake, they hate me."

"Nonsense," he whispered while his hands made gentle circles along her spine. Her slender form silhouetted against the nebulous moonlight, seemed fragile, child like. She turned towards him; her face drawn and pale seemed to increase her age by ten years. His heart was breaking, his children were the cause of this severe transition, and he knew it was pointless denying the truth. They did hate her and there was not a damn thing he could do about it. Tenderly he lifted her chin with one finger, "We can work this out Cass, we can get through it, it's as you say; they need a little more time."

She shuddered; his caress was causing involuntary goose bumps all over her body. "Time is no longer the important element, the ugly truth is, whether we give them six months or six years, they are never going to accept me as your wife or their friend, let alone stepmother." She turned back facing the night, hot tears scalded her eyes. Jake tried to swallow, but something, perhaps his heart, was caught in his throat. She had tried so hard, so damned hard, how could he blame her for giving up. Yet nothing on the face of this earth could prompt him to let her go. Encircling her within his strong arms, and allowing the outlet she required he comforted her silently. When the crying had finally subsided he rocked her gently backwards and forwards trying to instill the need in him for her not to give up.

"I can't let you walk away from our relationship because of a few minor setbacks. I'll do anything to prevent that, even if it means going to Rae and insisting she take the children."

The idea that we would do that brought a second flow of tears, and at that moment she knew the depth of his love for her, she could not leave him, not now. "No Jake, I could never let you do that. When the children finally go to their Mother, it will be because she has asked for them, not because of me. Now that I know I have your strength, your support to fall back on, I know we can work it out." Jake traced his finger around her nipple, and then gently lowered her beside him. She quivered beneath his touch as he replaced his finger with his tongue teasing her already erect nipple. His hands moved across every avenue of her body causing her to writhe beneath him until she couldn't stand his teasing any longer. "Take me Jake," she whispered urgently, "Take me now!" He penetrated her easily, his arousal filling her desire. Once their passion abated, they lay locked in each others' arms until the tranquility of sleep claimed them.

Chapter 7

The first golden streaks of dawn rose proudly over the sleeping houses of Wanneroo. A few stars still twinkled dimly, reluctant to hide their jeweled auras of the night. Summer lingered unwilling to yield to the onset of autumn. It was going to be a perfect day. It was their wedding day. Nothing could go wrong today, nothing. Cassie glanced towards Jake; he slept soundly oblivious to the marvels of this glorious sunrise.

It had been forty eight hours since he had rocked her gently, soothing her like a child. Nothing had deterred her since then, not since he had been willing to relinquish his children for her could Dane or anyone else mar her new found feeling of security. The past two weeks had been a nightmare, one trauma after another. Her total despair at being unable to please them or gain their acceptance made her want to scream and run. In fact, the night Jake had come to her, was the night she was going to concede defeat, call everything off and flee like a wounded starling. But now everything had changed, he wanted her more than his kids, she didn't need to try any longer, the battle was over and in effect she had won.

Throwing the covers back, she slid softly from the bed to the window. The last stars had completely faded, as had her fears and doubts and now as the sun enveloped its warmth around the new day, she knew she had a future with Jake.

Cassie had already showered and was dressing into her wedding outfit, a soft pink taffeta suit, when Jake finally stirred. He opened his eyes and smiled at the vision she presented. The finely tailored skirt molded around her slim hips like a glove, an elegant but not overly promiscuous split at the back, revealed her long shapely legs to just above the knee. A short sleeved, v necked bodice plunged deeply to the waist; a single button reunited the sides beneath her breasts, only to be recaptured by a ruffle, giving the design a 50's appearance; which was further enhanced by a white high necked semi lace blouse. A delicate spray of white baby breath and red carnations embellished the shoulder.

He watched fascinated as she ran the flat of her hands over her smooth stomach, then turned from one side to the other front of the full length mirror braced against the wall.

Sensing his appraisal, she turned; he lay motionless with his face alight with amusement, a cheeky grin from ear to ear. He whistled and she turned away toying with a make believe piece of thread on the skirt, a tinge of pink creeping into her cheeks giving away her embarrassment. "I was just checking for any last minute alterations."

Sitting up and propping himself against the pillows his folded his hands behind his head, the saucy grin remaining. He knew perfectly well she had completed all the alterations days ago, he was aware also of her reservations about the style. "You look beautiful Cass, a picture luscious enough to frame in 24ct gold."

That was the most ridiculous statement he had made, yet she blushed and laughed, "Well thank you sir. But don't you think it's just a teeny bit old fashioned," she closed one eye and brought her finger and thumb together in a wee gesture.

Knitting his fingers, he pushed his arms palms first toward her in a profound stretch, and yawned, "Nope! It's perfect, like you." She moved to his side of the bed and positioned a kiss on the tip of his nose. He reached up instinctively wrapping his locked hands behind her neck. Any endeavor at keeping her face inches from his failed when an untimely knock on the door broke the moment. She stood as Dane strutted in. The boy eyed her appearance, "Is that your wedding dress?" She nodded. "It's nice." Cassie couldn't help but blush, this was a compliment, and since it came from Dane she had to control her urge to whirl and drop in a dead faint. Even Jake looked surprised. So astounded was he, he didn't have the heart to chastise his son at not waiting to be acknowledged before entering. "I'm sorry to disturb you, but the caterers are on the phone."

An overt glance passed between them, they had been so engrossed with each other, they hadn't even heard the phone ring. Without further comment, Cassie left to take the call. Dane turned to follow, but Jake stopped him. "That was a very nice thing you said to Cassie son, I'm proud of you."

The boy shrugged, "It was the truth," he turned and left quickly before his father could see the smile of pleasure that curled his lips.

Jake was showering when she returned to the room. She removed her outfit, laying it carefully across the bed, and then stepped into a pair of jeans and sweat shirt. She would redress closer to eleven the time of the ceremony, which was still three hours away. Jake emerged from the steamy en-suite, a towel hung loosely around his hips. "What did the caterers want?"

"They just wanted to confirm the amount of guests we're expecting," she waved her hand in dismissal, "something to do with the entrees."

In the kitchen Dane prepared four bowls of cereal. The muffled voices of his Father and Cassie behind their bedroom door seemed to fill the otherwise silent house with deafening clarity. 'I'm proud of you.' Jakes' words echoed through his head, and all he had done was say Cassie's outfit was nice. For the first time since she had come into their life, he felt the bond had and his Father once shared begin to re-develop. Such a small sentence, yet it had obviously meant so much. He smiled to himself, perhaps if he stopped being a jerk and made an effort to be pleasant to her; … his thoughts were interrupted as three sleepy siblings entered the room, their hungry tummies seeking breakfast. Jeffrey grimaced at his bowl of corn flakes, "Is that all we get this morning. How come Cassie didn't make pancakes?"

Sometimes Dane had a hard time remembering Jeffrey was only very young, he snapped with impatience, "Get real stupid, today she marries Dad, she hasn't got time to cook dumb pancakes."

The young boy pinched his cheeks pulling down his bottom eye lids and poked out his tongue in a rather unseemly manner. Dane sighed, "such a child." Carly giggled at the sight of Jeff's grotesque face before asking her older brother for a pair of scissors. "What do you need them for?" he questioned still miffed by Jeff's action.

"I'm going to help Felicity make Betsy a dress for the marrying."

"You mean wedding," he corrected, removing the lethal object from the top cupboard, "Make sure you're very careful with these, we don't want any accidents, especially today."

"Yes Dane," she mocked. "Do you know where Cassie keeps the material?"

Sitting in front of his bowl, he heaped a large spoonful of cereal in his mouth, milk oozed between his lips, and he wiped it away with the back of his hand before answering, "In her room I guess, now eat your breakfast before it gets all soggy."

Cassie and Jake walked arm in arm, just as they were finishing, she smiled with approval at Danes initiative, "Thanks for getting them organized, I really didn't have the inclination to cook this morning."

Dane smiled sheepishly, a deep red was creeping into his cheeks, he rose and turned to the sink before she noticed, "That's alright, I figured you'd be busy doing other things." Being nice to her was really rather easy, he could even get used to it; "I'll make you and Dad some too, if you like, and then clean up so you can get ready."

Jake completely speechless at this new found co-operation, glanced at Cassie, her mouth was parted slightly as she faltered for words. She looked at him and shrugged. This was such a turnabout in attitude; it was very hard to accept. Finally, after a moment's pause, she turned back to Dane, "That would be lovely; I'll have some toast and coffee please."

Jake stood behind his son, his arms automatically encompassed the lad, and "I'll have the same." Then without thinking, kissed Dane on the back of the head; "OMG; YUK Dad!!" he complained, recoiling instantly. His father threw his arms in the air; "Sorry, I keep forgetting you're too old to be kissed; by me anyway."

They lingered over breakfast until ten o'clock, this was the first meal Dane had cooked them, and even though it was only toast, would most likely be the last. Finally Cassie pushed her chair back, "Well, we have to be at the Council Gardens in one hour, so I guess it's time to get ready."

Jake concurred, he looked around the kitchen, everything had been cleaned up, obviously, whilst they had been having their leisurely breakfast, Dane had gone by his word, unnoticed. In fact when the girls walked in dressed and ready, she nearly fell over her lip. This had been the most incredible morning, their future as a family was definitely looking better. She was about to say as much, when Felicity pulled the doll she had been keeping for a surprise from behind her back and thrust it towards her. "See the new dress Carly made for Betsy." The world began to spin; saliva filled her mouth while her stomach was close to rejecting her breakfast. The soft pink rag wrapped around the doll and tied with a shoe lace looked all too familiar. No! It couldn't be!! Dropping to the Childs level, she grabbed the doll; this wasn't possible, it couldn't be happening. With deliberate slowness she asked carefully, "Where did you get the material for this lovely dress?"

"From your room, Dane said '" Cassie didn't hear the rest, she waited for no explanations, the doll was dropped, and she was gone. Jake, unaware of the significance of a piece of cloth followed. The ensuing scream, brought him running the last few feet. "What the hell?!"

"Look at it! Jake, look at what they've done!" Tears cascaded down her face. He looked blankly at the skirt she held before him, a gaping rectangle cut from the centre.

Swallowing hard, he tried to remain calm, "Can you fix it?"

Flinging the ruined garment at him, she turned and cleared the dressing table with the back of her hand. Perfume bottles shattered sending a myriad of aromas into the air, *"Of course I can't FIX IT!! " Who do you think I am, Superwoman!?"* He motioned towards her, but she held out a warning arm, *"Don't come near me! That's it Jake, I can't take anymore."*

Hearing the commotion, Dane had skulked quietly to the doorway. Cassie spotted him, took three strides to face him, then without warning, raised her right arm and brought her hand heavily across his left cheek. His head hit the door frame on impact. *"You little bastard! It was all your doing wasn't it!?* she screamed at him, then lowering her voice whispered: "And to think I actually believed you were sincerely being nice. But the whole time you were setting me up, weren't you?!"

Jake tried to intervene, "Cass, please, I'm sure he..," but he was cut short by her acid tongue. *"Fool! Can't you see what sort of human being you're raising!? He's evil, the devils' advocate. It wouldn't matter who you wanted to marry, he'd play the same cruel tricks. What he needs is a bloody good hiding, but you're such a wimp, you wouldn't even know how!"*

This was too much; he grabbed her and began to shake her violently, until her hysteria subsided. Cassie threw herself across the bed and continued to sob softly into the pillow. Jake grabbed Dane by the scruff of his neck and dragged him into the corridor, shutting her muffled sobs behind him. "Tell me you had nothing to do with this!" His voice was like a volcano waiting to erupt. The boy starred at his Father, his head ached and the welt on his face still stung from her blow. Tears were biting his eyes, but he refused to cry. His first impression of her had been correct, there was absolutely no way he would accept her into this house now. She could go straight to hell. Jake shook him roughly, *"Answer me damn it!!"* Dane remained silent, a silence Jake considered as admission. The boy flinched and cowered when he raised his hand, but he made no contact. Instead he shoved him into the wall, *"You're pathetic; you know that!"* He shook his head in disgust and walked away. After a moment of trying to compose himself, Dane finally yielded to the blinding tears and fled sobbing from the house.

Jake positioned himself next to the phone, one hand was placed on his hip, the other propped against the wall. His head hung low beside his outstretched arm. Well, may as well get it over with, there would be no wedding today and he would have to do a lot of fast talking to ensure there would be one in the future, but for right now, he had a few calls to make.

Picking up the receiver, he dialed the Marriage Celebrant. A husky voice answered, "Hello, Phelps speaking."

"Mr. Phelps it's Jake Marshall." His voice wavered, a sudden urge to cry like a baby threatened to spew forth, "I'm sorry, but my fiancée has, er, come down with something. I'm afraid we're going to have to cancel the ceremony."

There was a brief pause, "I see. Good job you rang when you did, I was just on my way out the door. Nothing too serious I hope?" He sounded earnest enough, but Jake could tell he was a little more than peeved. But then who could blame him. It was extremely late notice, not to mention the $150 he would be foregoing. "No; just the flu or something."

David Phelps laughed, he had been marrying people for fifteen years, and every time there was a cancellation it was due to the 'flu or something'. "Maybe nerves, do you think?"

Jake far from jovial, "Yeah maybe," he responded flatly, "Goodbye."

One down, one to go, then he would have to drive the seven minutes to the Gardens and tell his guests. Fortunately there wasn't too many, hopefully they would understand. He commenced dialing then stopped, what was the number of the damn caterer. Oh crap, oh what the hell let them bring it. It would be too late to stop them now anyway. Besides, he would still have to pay whether he cancelled or not, so they may as well eat as much as they can, and freeze what's left.

"I'm sorry, I over reacted." Her voice startled him; he almost dropped the receiver he was cradling. A further shock took hold when he turned to face her. She was wearing a pale blue satin and chiffon overlay dress, very plain in style but intricately cut. The long sheer sleeves met at the wrists with a single pearl button. Although he had never seen it on her before, he had seen it hanging under a plastic sheath in the wardrobe. A lump caught in his throat and for a fleeting second he was glad the other garment had been ruined, this dress was far more stunning. Rather than restyling her hair, she had left it long; the silky strands flowed over her shoulders like a waterfall. Pale blue dust adorned her long lashed eye lids, enhancing her sapphire eyes even more. He cleared his throat, what did this all mean. "Well don't just stand there like a lump, get dressed, we have a wedding to attend."

Her bewitching eyes held him spellbound, he stammered, "But, but, I've just cancelled the Celebrant."

"Well I'll just have to ring him back while you get ready."

Chapter 8

Long hot summer days and oppressive nights had taken its toll on all of them. Today was their anniversary, and as with last year, autumn refused to come easing the cruel and sweltering heat. Cassie blinked away a tear, some anniversary, they had been arguing for weeks, and every morning she would wake with Jake already gone into the garden. Today had been no exception. She had thought, or rather hoped, it would be different. Wiping the perspiration from her brow, she bent, scooping up another load of washing and threw it carelessly into the machine. She could see Jake in the distance from the laundry window, talking to one of his staff. A light rain like gossamer mist had begun to fall making the humidity worse. Moving to the kitchen, she opened the fridge and withdrew a large pitcher of iced tea. Closing the door with her elbow, she leaned back against it, absorbing the coolness from the heavy metal door. This was ridiculous; she couldn't even remember what they were arguing about. Well, one thing was for certain, and that was, she was going to have to be the one to make amends. Perhaps a dinner party in honour of their first year of wedded bliss. Cassie chuckled to herself, BLISS, what a joke. It had been horrendous. Maybe she should change that to a Wake!! "Now Cass old girl, get serious," she mentally chastised.

She would ring Skye and invite her and Roger, and then she would race off to the supermarket and buy something really special to cook. But what? She scratched her head with her free hand, Jake would be coming in for his lunch soon, best she organize something for him to eat first, and then decide what to have for dinner on the way to the store.

The largest shopping mall in Wanneroo had its' usual hordes of people busying themselves with the weekly groceries, or simply lingering in the air conditioned building seeking relief from this murderous weather. Cassie cursed under her breath at having to park in the most further car bays. The fine rain continued to fall steadily around her, caressing her face with cool seductive fingers on its final descent to the ground. A woman in a red maternity dress hastily crossed her path, almost tripping her. Her head was buried beneath a large umbrella and bent towards the ground, but, there was something about her, perhaps the wisps of red hair just barely visible, or even the way she walked. Cassie felt her heart palpitate, and when the woman quickened her pace so did she. Someone from afar called out her name, she turned and swore. It was Mrs. Bradford one of the Mothers from the girls' kindergarten, waving frantically and approaching rapidly. This irritating Amazon of a woman had a tendency to prattle on for ages if you let her, and she only had an hour to get what she wanted before she had to pick up the girls. Cassie didn't alter her pace, she smiled briefly, waved back and turned away, leaving the insulted Mrs. Bradford slightly miffed. However, in the few seconds it took to accomplish this, the mysterious vision in red had vanished.

Irate mothers with screaming babies and whining toddlers bustled about impatiently, while the combined odour of damp clothes and cheap perfume gave her the urge to throw up.

Cassie made her way to the meat department, and was deliberating on what type of steak to have, when a flash of red caught her eye. Grabbing a large pack of porter house steak, she followed. Up one aisle, down the next, Cassie kept even pace, but without seeing her face, she couldn't be sure. Finally the woman turned side on. Apart from being very pregnant, there was no mistaking that profile, the perfectly straight nose and naturally long eyelashes were her best features. It was indeed Philyce.

Cassie remained obscure for a while; her friends last words resounding in her head, "And should you ever happen to see me in the Street, please do me the courtesy of doing the same." But then she had said Street, not SHOP. What the hell, she had to try; besides if ever she needed a friend it was now. This last year had been a bitch. Many times she could have used a friendly shoulder to cry on. Skye had been cordial enough, always offering her ear, but she was a fair bit older, and Cassie felt she couldn't confide everything in her. She couldn't explain to her how she loathed the air Dane breathed, nor could she mention how inadequate their love making had become recently. No Skye had been with Jake too long, she really needed Phil.

This was going to be difficult, swallowing her pride was one thing Cassie was not very good at; she took a deep breath and approached with as much nonchalance as she could muster, "Hello Philyce." The woman spun around surprised, almost dropping the jar she was holding.

"Well! As I live and breathe, Cassie! Fancy meeting you way out here in the sticks. How the hell are you?"

Cassie withheld her relief, that wasn't so hard, and at least now she knew Phil was speaking to her again. She shrugged her shoulders and sighed, "So, so." Then pointing to her friend's protruding stomach, grinned impishly, "I can see you're doing alright, although slightly fatter than when I saw you last."

Philyce laughed, "Only slightly?! How kind, I'm enormous and you know it."

An uncomfortable moment lapsed, with both women failing for words, finally Cassie asked the obvious, "Aren't you going to tell me who, when and how long to go?"

Embarrassment seemed to radiate from her flushed cheeks, "Don Averling."

"Your boss?"

"Uh ha. Can you believe it? He popped the question right out of the blue. I think it was as much of a surprise to him as it was to me. We've been married just over a year and junior here is due in about seven weeks. What about you?"

"I married Jake. In fact it's our anniversary today."

"Wow, the man with all the kids. How's it going?"

Cassie shrugged, this was neither the time nor the place; "Phil, about what happened before, I'm so sorry."

Their eyes locked, she took Cassie's hand, "I know, so am I."

Tears stung her eyes, she blinked them away, "Listen, I'm having a little dinner party tonight to celebrate our anniversary, I don't suppose there's any chance of you and Don coming?"

Philyce didn't hesitate, "Sure, love to."

Her surprise was obvious, Phil laughed, "Don't look so shocked, just tell me where and what time."

Reaching into her purse, she extracted one of Jake's business cards and handed it to her friend, "Say seven."

Cassie couldn't believe how easy this had all been, she wanted desperately to stay and talk more, but she still had to pick up the girls. At least Jeff was old enough to ride, so he was no problem, and Dane, well he wasn't worth thinking about. "Well as much as I'd love to catch up on all the gossip, I'm afraid I'll have to fly. I have to pick up the girls from Kindergarten."

"Sure, I understand, so Jake has twins?"

Cassie laughed, "Oh heavens no. Actually Felicity goes to play group which adjoins the Kindergarten, so I have a habit of connecting the two together. See you at seven."

Jake ambled in for lunch. A note on the table informed him where she was. He glanced at the sandwiches covered with cling wrap she had left him, and pushed them aside. The way things were going between them at the moment, left him without an appetite. He reached into his pocket and pulled out a small box; it contained a delicate pair of diamond stud earrings. It was her anniversary present, so why the hell hadn't he given them to her this morning, instead of bolting into the garden like a bull at a gate.

Pouring himself a large glass of iced tea, he reflected over the last year. What a year it had been. It started with their wedding; Dane had vanished from sight, so they had to go without him, then when they came back for the reception, they found him curled up on his bed like a wounded puppy, and no amount of cajoling would bring him out of his room, even Cassies' apology had no effect. Then there was the honeymoon. Unable to afford the luxury of along honeymoon, they decided to spend several days at an Inn at Yanchep which was only a few miles away. Less than twelve hours after their arrival, Skye had rung to advise her husband had broken his ankle and could not manage the market garden for him as planned, nor could she keep the children at her house with him home. When he rang Rae to ask if she would take them, she had flatly refused, apparently her art was more important than his stupid honeymoon. So they had come back and resumed normal duties.

His glass drained he poured another. Why was trying to settle down in a normal family relationship so bloody hard. It was Dane, purely and simply. The boy was unapproachable, he seemed to be locked in his own little world and nobody could get in and he certainly wasn't coming out. He blamed Cassie for Dustys' death, claiming she had given him bad meat. Even the word of the Veterinarian that he had simply died from natural causes, could not convince him. In fact a week later, they had taken the children to a nearby lake to feed the ducks, whereby Dane accidently on purpose, pushed her in. That had been the last straw, he had given him ten of the best across the backside, yet even that hadn't brought him down. Instead it seemed to have an adverse effect; Dane became more determined, withdrawn and difficult. Jake inhaled deeply; everything had become so bloody complicated. And now, he and Cassie were arguing; over what? It had been that long since they had a decent conversation without slinging the proverbial at each other, he couldn't even remember.

The car pulled into the drive, the engine roared once, then off. Cassie was home. He ran his fingers through his hair, time to depart before they started on each other again. Carly and Felicity ran in through the back door. "Hi Dad, can we watch Bugs Bunny, Cassie got us a video," the older girl squealed with delight.

"Sure baby, here give it to me; I'll set it up for you." This was very unusual; Cassie never let the children watch television in the afternoon, claiming it was a waste of brain power. Only if she was in an extremely good mood did she ever relent.

"What's up Doc" echoed from the lounge room as he walked back into the kitchen; she was unloading a bag of groceries. "Hi honey, can you finish in the garden reasonably early today, we're having company for dinner."

Jake smiled, this was a refreshing change of tone, "No problem, who?"

Leaving the few unpacked items on the table, she moved towards him. His heart raced when she folded her arms around his neck, and kissed him deeply. This was the first expression of passion in weeks, and he was reluctant to let it pass. Instinctively, his hand made its way up her leg, under cotton shift and into her panties. Breaking free, she stepped back,

"Not now honey, I have too much to do." The disappointed line of his mouth made her laugh, "Relax we've got all night to do that."

He smiled, trying to ignore the ache in his groin from her teasing, "Promise." She nodded. "Who's coming again?

"Well Skye and Roger for one. And do you remember me telling you about Philyce, the girl that came from Sydney with me?" He tapped his lip with his finger, "Vaguely. Is that the one you had the argument with?" She nodded; as to date she still hadn't told him the truth of that confrontation, nor did she intend to; "That's the one, well I met her at the shop today, we sort of made amends and she and her husband are coming."

"I see," he purposely spoke with a drawl, "And tell me Mrs. Marshall, what exactly is the occasion?" She punched him playfully in the chest, "You know very well," and kissed him again.

"Oh yes, that's right, its someone's birthday today," he teased reaching into his pocket. Cassie decided to play along with his little game, "Yes, I'm sure it is, somewhere; most likely many someone's as a matter of fact."

Handing her the small box, he pretended to be coy, "Happy anniversary darling." Lifting the lid, she responded with a gasp, "Oh Jake, they're absolutely beautiful. I take back all the horrible thoughts I had about you this morning."

"I'm not even going to ask." The teasing moment passed, when he noticed the blood drain from her face, she began to sway; he grabbed her arm and led her to the chair. "What's wrong honey? Was it something I said?" He was trying to keep the flippant mood going and she smiled briefly, but waves of nausea were threatening to make her vomit. "I just feel a little queasy."

Perspiration beaded across her brow, he wiped it with a handkerchief, "I think I'd better get you to the Doctor, you look dreadful Cass."

She reached, out grabbing his arm, "NO! I'll be alright, just give me a minute. His face was lined with concern, she tried to reassure him, "Really honey, it's nothing. You go back to work. I'll lie down for a little while, I'll be fine."

"Are you sure?" She nodded, "Yes, I'm positive. Now go back to work, or you won't be finished until late."

Cassie lay on the bed, her hands folded across her stomach. She smiled; she had known for several weeks about the tiny life growing within her womb, but she couldn't tell him, not yet, this was his anniversary present. When she first learned the news, she felt she was going to explode with joy; she wanted to shout it to him the moment she returned from the Doctor. The thought of keeping it a secret until now almost drove her crazy, but she pictured the look on his face when she tells him; and knew it would be the ultimate anniversary gift. Nothing could compare to the gift of life. Sadly the arguments had started and then keeping the secret became easy.

When Jake came in around 6:30 Cassie had fed the children and was doing their dishes. She was dressed in her wedding dress. He stood behind her and pushing her flowing hair aside, kissed her softly on the nape of the neck, "How do you feel now?"

Peering at him over her shoulder, she grinned, "I'm fine. I think I was just hungry, I've had an apple and I'm ok now, honestly!" she lied. "Now go and get ready our guests will be here soon and you're still not ready, go, go …!" she waved him out the door.

He saluted, "Yes boss!" The sound of silence suddenly became very deafening, "Where are the kids?"

"They're all in the boys' room holding a séance."

Jake grimaced, "I don't think that's a very good idea Cass.

Rae was always poking around with that wretched thing, and sometimes it got pretty spooky."

"Relax Jake, they're amateurs. I doubt very much if they know what they're doing, besides, it's all a load of hogwash anyway."

Chapter 9

Dane prepared the Ouija board, while the others sat around him in a circle on the floor. "Right guys, now we all have to place one finger very lightly on the glass."

Jeffrey groaned, "This is dumb and boring; why can't we watch television?"

Dane threw him a warning glance; "Stop whining. I already told you, I want to see if there's any way of getting rid of HER. Besides, SHE organized a dinner party with her friends, and we're not welcome in there because the TV would make too much noise, and that would interfere with their conversation."

They sat in position for a few minutes, Carly started to giggle, Dane grew impatient, "Quiet!"

Jeffrey sighed, "This is really, really dumb!" his brother flicked his ear, the small boy cried out, "Ouch! That hurt!"

"It was meant to; now shut up! How do you expect anything to happen if you're going to grizzle all the time?" A moment later, the glass began to move slightly, Jeffrey gasped; "You're pushing that Dane!" Danes' face paled, "Shush, I AM NOT!" Round and round the glass began to rotate, Felicity pulled away when the glass started to move faster, "I'm scared!" Dane ignored her, "Is there anybody here?" he asked slowly, his voice quivering slightly. They all stared as the glass moved to the letters Y E S. Please identify yourself," he asked. Having sat through countless séances with his Mother, he was reasonably familiar with the procedure. Slowly the glass moved around the board pausing briefly at each letter, B..A..B..Y.. Dane stared speechless for a moment; "Baby; what does that mean?" Again the glass moved under three fingers and spelled BABY. The fear in his voice was becoming apparent, "Please identify yourself?" he asked for the second time.

Ignoring the question the glass moved and came to rest in front of Carly; then after a few seconds began its course again, their quivering fingers pushing the glass to the letters: D A N G E R. "Make it stop Dane, I'm scared!!" the small girl pleaded. Dane by now was terrified himself, and didn't need to be asked twice. "OK everybody take your finger off the glass." They obeyed and the glass as though released from pressure, fell over.

The six adults sat around the dining table, the intimate glow from the candles sent shadows dancing around the room. Cassie glanced at Jake next to her; he was conversing in depth with Don. Sensing her appraisal he glimpsed toward her briefly, winking before returning his attention to his guest. Everything was going so well, even the dreadful heat couldn't put a damper on this evening.

Cassie was watching her friends intently, absorbing every detail; she couldn't help but be amused by the contrast in shapes, sizes and personalities. Her mouth curved involuntarily at the picture they presented. Skye round and jolly, Roger tall and lanky, with dominance oozing from his staid face. If he said jump, she asked how high. Philyce caught her attention, and hiding her mouth behind her hand she motioned her head towards Don, her perfect lips mimed B.O.R.E. Cassie laughed softly, how true. From the moment he had been introduced he had monopolized the conversation, talking about family law and the new Mercedes he had just bought, neither of which interested any of them. Poor Jake, he was being the perfect host, listening with pretended interest to the entire dribble. She eyed Don intently, what Philyce saw in him, was beyond her. Short; fat; a receding hair line that left the front of his head shining like a bowling ball; immaculately dressed in a three piece suite; which she guessed was definitely not purchased from K Mart, and with all the gold dripping from his neck and wrists, not to mention the diamond rings adorning his fingers; he actually reminded her of the main character in a movie she once saw; the title she couldn't remember. His thin lips worked unceasingly, so in order to save Jake's ear, she decided not to delay dinner.

They feasted on garlic prawns, peppered steak with roast potatoes and Caesar salad, and had just completed a strawberry mousse with whipped cream, when Cassie decided now was the time to make her announcement. Slipping one hand into Jakes, she raised the other in a bid for attention. "Excuse me everyone," and once silence ensued, continued, "I have a present for my husband whom I would like to share with all of you." When he squeezed her hand, for a brief moment she thought he already knew, so when she noticed his face was a mask of curiosity, she exhaled with relief. Locking eyes, she raised her glass of water to him, "I have no material gift wrapped with pretty paper, but in late October I'm going to present you with a baby: happy anniversary darling!!"

"Why does there always have to be so many ads?" Felicity complained bitterly.

Dane stretched and yawned, "Just to give us kids the shi …," he stopped when he saw Jeffrey wave a warning finger at him. Uncrossing his legs, he rose from the floor where they had all been sitting watching Superman on the portable television. "Who wants a snack or something?" *Me*, they all echoed. "OK I'll go and see if I can score something from the bit.." Jeffrey's finger moved again, "witch," he corrected.

Dane quietly tiptoed past the dining room and was silently rummaging through the pantry in the kitchen when she began her announcement. He froze; then peered unnoticed through the adjoining door; they started laughing and cheering, a bald fat man began patting his Father on the back. Nobody saw him, nor saw the fear in his eyes, nor felt the hatred in his heart.

Jake cradled Cassie in his arms as they lay in bed that night. He ran his hand up her naked leg resting it gently on her stomach. "You nearly blew me away with that announcement tonight. How long have you known?" Feathering her fingers along his cheek, she smiled, "A few weeks. Are you angry I didn't tell you before?" Removing her hand from his face, he gently kissed each finger. "No, I'm not angry, just surprised you could keep it a secret that long."

"Well; for sure it wasn't easy," she confessed, "although, I must admit our lack of communication helped. How do you think the children will take the news?" He shrugged; that was a very good question, unfortunately, one he didn't know the answer to.

She placed her hand on her stomach, "You know, they say babies can hear their Mother's voice and feel what she feels almost from the time of conception. I've been singing lullaby's to him and speaking to him when nobodies around. He already knows how much we love and cherish him." Jake looked surprised "HE" she nodded, "yes it's a boy; I'm certain of it."

Cassie was up and in the kitchen preparing breakfast by the first streaks of dawn. They had decided to inform the children of the new baby first thing, so had considered a special breakfast was in order to soften the blow, might be appropriate. Of course, there was always the possibility they would be delighted, but she doubted it very much, especially Dane. The aroma of bacon, eggs, pancakes and blueberry muffins wafted down the corridor. Jake came in with his nose in the air, "Yum, we'll have all the neighbors knocking at the door for an invitation" he laughed. "What's the occasion that signifies a breakfast fit for a king?"

Handing him a cup of coffee she sat down "It's a bribe; to soothe the savage beast or rather beasts." Jake pulled up a chair beside her, "Oh I see, you think they'll take it that badly huh?"

She smiled and sighed, "I'd put money on it. I really hope I'm being over sensitive but given the past year; especially with Dane." she shrugged "oh don't let me be negative; I really hope they'll ALL be as happy as we are!"

The girls were already at the table and scoffing the feast when Jeffrey and Dane finally appeared. The younger boy squealed with delight, "Wow, blueberry muffins AND pancakes!" Dane however, poured himself a glass of orange juice and headed for the back door. A deep frown creased Jake's brow, "Where do you think you're going son?"

"Outside," his voice held an edge of defiance, which left Jake with the feeling of an impending argument about to erupt. "*Really!* And what about breakfast? Cassie has gone to a lot of trouble, so I strongly suggest it would be in your best interest to sit down and eat something." Dane ignored him and just kept walking "Not hungry" was all he said.

Here it was not quite eight o'clock and already another difficult day with this tenacious teenager in the making. Only for Cassie's sake did Jake keep himself in check, "Oh I think you are, now sit down. Besides I have some news for all of you." The boy held his Father's gaze briefly, and then glanced towards Cassie, who with her back to them was folding tea towels at the sink. He already knew what the news was, and he didn't care to hear it again, however, Jake's eyes had gone black, a warning he knew only too well, so with painstaking slowness he moved to the table and sat down. Arms folded, he sat silently trying to ignore the growling in his stomach and the delicious aromas filling the room. He looked at his Father, who was sipping his coffee and eyeing him speculatively over the rim of the cup. He was going to make him wait, the bastard was deliberately dragging this out, torturing him with the food he was adamant he would not eat. Finally after five minutes, Dane yielded and helped himself to some muffins.

Jake smiled, "Right, now I will tell you our news," he reached for Cassie, pulling her from the sink on to his lap, and feeling her body stiffen slightly, patted her leg for reassurance. "Cassie told me last night she is going to have a baby!" They looked around the table at the children waiting for some form of response. All with the exception of Dane had stopped eating and were staring at them with eyes like saucers. Jeffrey broke the silence, "Wow! A baby." Carly swallowed a mouthful of unchewed food, almost choking in her haste to speak. "Will I be able to hold it?"

Cassie, who had been holding her breath, instinctively exhaled, and smiled with relief, "Of course. In fact I'm counting on all of you to help me look after him or her." Felicity smiled, "I'll help you. If you want to, the baby can sleep with me instead of Betsy.

The very idea that this small child was prepared to oust her beloved doll in favor of the baby was quite a privilege, which left Cassie with the task of refusing in a way that wouldn't hurt her feelings.

"That's very kind of you sweetheart, but don't you think Betsy might become terribly upset?" The child thought about it for a moment, "Yes, I guess she would. Do you think the baby would mind if I kept Betsy instead?"

Cassie shook her head "Oh no sweetheart, I'm quite sure the baby wouldn't mind at all."

Dane pushed his chair back the sound of which brought Jake's attention back to him, "So what do you think about it Dane?" Ignoring his Father's question, he glanced passed him at Cassie, "Can I be excused?"

Jake opened his mouth, but she spoke first, "Of course." When he was out of view, she arose from Jake's lap and sat beside him. "I know what you were going to say, but it would have been useless. Dane's not a baby anymore Jake, he has a mind of his own; and obviously he doesn't care for our news, so the best thing is to leave it."

Jake ran his fingers through his hair, it was a moment before he spoke, "You know, I really don't understand you sometimes. Dane has been a little bastard to you from day one, yet you always seem to jump to his defence. In fact the only time you didn't was on our wedding day and that's probably the worst I've seen you react with him."

She smiled, "Like I told you before, you can't make him like me. His attitude is deliberate, it's a form of punishment and every time you get cross, he considers he has won that round. The best thing is to let him work out his aggression his own way, if for no other reason than to keep the peace and make things more pleasant around here."

Jake rose from the table, "Well that may be, but I'll tell you this Cass, I'm almost at the end of my tether, too much more provocation from him, and I swear, I'll send the little prick packing."

Chapter 10

Albany Highway was congested as normal, motorists turning right causing major hold ups. Cassie cursed under her breath, and glanced at her passenger, "I hate this damn road." Philyce smiled, "Well, you did insist on buying your maternity and baby clothes from the same place I did.

"You didn't tell me we had to come to bloody Cannington. Whatever possessed you to come way out here?" The pretty redhead sighed; Cassie had started complaining the moment she sat behind the wheel, and after fifty minutes of non- stop ear bashing her patience was wearing thin. "You're forgetting I lived in Victoria Park with Don when I became pregnant, which is only fifteen minutes away."

Cassie bit her bottom lip, "I'm sorry, it's not your fault I feel so lousy." Morning sickness had commenced three weeks earlier, and now at ten weeks along, she could see the thickening of her waist and notice the very slight roundness of her stomach, but of course nobody else could. As far as she was concerned this was grossly unfair, after all she was a sick as a dog most mornings, she certainly felt pregnant, therefore shouldn't she look pregnant? It had been Phil's idea to start buying maternity clothes, "Even if you're not showing yet, hopping into flowing dresses will make you feel as though you are," she had said. The onset of April had brought the cool welcome fingers of autumn, finally easing the oppressive balmy haze of summer. Rain began to fall in heavy drops, "Great; that's all I need." The traffic lights ahead turned amber, Cassie eased her foot on the brake, "Have you noticed we've hit almost every red light since …" her friend moaned softly, and paused mid sentence to look at her. Philyce had turned deathly pale, her face was creased with pain, "Good Lord, you look awful, what's wrong?"

"Thanks for the compliment PAL; as a matter of fact I feel awful. My back is burning and I have a cramps.UH!" she gasped.

"What is it?!" Cassie cried alarmed by her friend's obvious discomfort. "It's this pain, and I think my water just broke." The light changed to green, Cassie felt as though her heart was hitting her ribs. Swerving into the right land she hit the accelerator and did an unauthorized U turn, heading them in the direction they had come. Irate motorists blew their horn and made unseemly gestures with their fingers, "Cassie what the hell are you doing?"

"What does it look like Phil, I'm taking you to the hospital. Try and relax, the pains have just started so we should have plenty of time." Philyce grabbed the dash board; her knuckles were turning white with the intensity of her grip as another pain seared through her body. "Actually, I don't think so. I've been having little pains since about three this morning."

Cassie glanced at her, mouth agape. "Oh for goodness sake!! Why the hell didn't you say something?"

"I've still got two weeks to go, so I just assumed the baby was stretching or something. It never occurred that it might be the start of labour."

"Honestly! Phil you can't be that dumb; babies don't follow calendars, and any idiot knows that." Changing into fourth gear, Cassie pushed the accelerator almost to the floor, "You'd better hang on, I would say we may not have that much time, and a long way to go. It could be a very bumpy ride."

How they managed to reach the hospital back in Wanneroo in one piece was a miracle. Even Cassie emerged from the car with legs like jelly. When Philyce was taken into the delivery room, Cassie rang Don at his office, which fortunately was only two blocks away.

Only thirty five minutes had lapsed from the time of their arrival to Don's announcement of the birth of his daughter. Cassie was elated and embraced him automatically, but when she felt his arms tightening around her waist, recoiled instantly. Their eyes met and for a moment she thought she read something in his heated gaze that should not be there. But when he smiled, it was gone. The only thing radiating from his face was that of a proud Father. "They are taking Phil through to her room, so if you'd like to come with me, I'll show where it is."

Cassie nodded and followed silently. Philyce sat propped against the pillows, her red hair shone like soft garnets against the white linen. Don moved to his wife and kissed her tenderly on the mouth. Cassie felt embarrassed. How could she have imagined he looked at her with anything other than friendship? His intimate kiss seemed to be lingering deliberately, she felt herself blush and became a little uncomfortable being there; she coughed with a childish awkwardness. It seemed to do the trick; he broke away abruptly, yet even though he was smiling, his eyes appeared to hold a hint of resentment. Philyce laughed, "Sorry, guess we got a little carried away," she patted the edge of the bed, "Come and sit here."

Cassie sat beside her and picked up her hand, "So tell me, is having a baby as bad as everyone says?"

"Well I guess that depends on what you would class bad

as. For me it was the most wonderful experience imaginable, and …" she giggled, "I can't wait to do it again." Don cleared his throat, "Well, we'll have to see about that. It may have been wonderful for you, but for me, it was nerve racking. In fact, if you don't mind I think I'll slip out and buy myself a cup of coffee."

Phil nodded, and as he closed the door whispered, "I'll be you a hundred dollars; he'll drink it outside the nursery."

For some unexplainable reason, Cassie had a sudden feeling of jealousy. Would Jake kiss her with such tenderness after the birth of their child? Would he find excuses to hover around the nursery and gaze lovingly at their new born? After all, after having four children already, surely the birth of his fifth would not harbor the same miraculous feeling it would for her. She shook her head back dismissing the webs of emotion clouding her mind. Of course he would. She was being ridiculous. Philyce squeezed her hand, "Penny for your thoughts."

Cassie smiled, "I was just trying to imagine what it will be like. Anyway I don't even know your daughter's name."

"Catherine Rose. And it won't work Cassandra Marshall. I know when you're trying to change the subject. You were thinking a lot more than that."

"Believe me, there was no subject to change." Phil studied her friend carefully, "You are such a bloody good liar," Cassie laughed, "Now I really am going to change the subject," she paused briefly, her voice became serious, "My friend, you will never know how much I missed you, and how glad I am I saw you at the supermarket." Philyce looked down, her long lashes blanketed her eyes and when she refocused on Cassie, they were filling with water, "Since it seems to be time for true confessions, I think you should know, I have one of my own," her voice wavered slightly, "The things you admitted that day hurt Cass, they hurt like hell. I left wondering how or more to the point why you would do that to me, and even though I deeply regretted the things I said to you almost immediately, I couldn't apologise or even let you explain for that matter, my pride wouldn't let me. There was a gaping hole in my heart that only our friendship could fill, but you had betrayed me, and since I knew sooner or later I would relent and come knocking on your door, I moved out and in with Don. Our relationship was purely platonic at first. Then he started looking at me in a different way and accidently touching me at every opportunity. I was repulsed at first, but then I thought, well why not, I didn't have you to turn to anymore and I hadn't made any other friends, well not that I could confide in anyway, so I gave in and slept with him. He started lavishing me with all kinds of expensive gifts: clothes, jewellery, silk underwear and numerous other things," she took a deep breath, "Don gave me a taste of the good life Cass, and when he asked me to marry him I jumped at the chance. But not because I loved him, because I didn't want to give all that away." She wiped away the tears with the back of her hand before continuing, "That's when I realized I was as guilty as you in manipulating and using people. Now comes the confession; our moving to Wanneroo was no coincidence. I traced your whereabouts from Mr. Tyson, and when Don said he wanted to start another practice North of the river, I practically begged him to come here. I had every intention of arriving on your door step one day, but as luck had it you saw me first, and I got to keep my pride."

Cassie had sat in silence trying to contain her tears. What a pitiful pair they were, her firstly for marrying Gavin to have a child and then even though she did love Jake having a child was her main concern, and Phil for marrying Don only for his money. It was ludicrous. As the tears began to spill, she began to laugh, a hysterical infectious laugh, which Philyce could not help but be caught in. They embraced each other, rocking with laughter. Anyone witnessing them at that moment would have thought they were both insane.

Jake sat in his favorite arm chair watching the cricket when his eyes weren't closed. The children were ferreting about in the garden so while Cassie shopped with Philyce he sat relaxing in the ambience of utter peace. The solitude of his momentary repose was inexcusably interrupted by the phone. The terseness of his tone indicated his disapproval, "Yes!"

"Jake, it's Rae, did I disturb you?"

"As a matter of fact, you did." He guessed by the ensuing silence she was deciding whether to hang up or continue.

"I heard along the grape vine, you're going to be a Father again. Do I congratulate or commiserate?"

He sighed heavily, he didn't need to ask who the grape vine was, "I'm exceptionally happy about it Rae."

Her voice seemed to grow flat, as though disappointed, "Well that's good, I can remember after Felicity was born, you were adamant there would be no more," she wavered, "Even though I wanted another baby."

"That was an entirely different situation, we already had four, Cassie is only twenty nine, it's only normal she would want a child of her own, and considering she is raising the children you SUPPOSEDLY wanted so desperately, I could hardly deny her that Motherly fulfillment.

The line was silent for a second, Rae bit her lip. He was doing it again, trying to make her feel guilty; normally she would have slammed the phone in his ear, but not this time. No way was she going to concede to his mental abuse, she would let that remark slide, "Yes of course, it's just that, well I was led to believe you were tricked into it, so I thought I'd just check for myself."

"I am going to be presumptuous here, and gather your source of information is Dane," she made no comment; "Yes I thought so. As you well know, Dane has a vivid imagination; he seems to see only what he wants to. I thank you for your concern, but I assure you I'm absolutely thrilled. Now if that's all, I bid you goodbye."

Rage grew in his gut like a volcano waiting to erupt, what bullshit she wanted another baby, absolute crap that's what it was. If she'd had her way after Felicity was born, he would have had a vasectomy. And as for Dane … he stormed to the back door and called him in, "I want to talk to you, the rest of you stay out there."

His voice left no room for argument or questions; they resumed their game whilst Dane ambled in. He had absolutely no idea what all this was about, but he strongly suspected it had something to do with his Stepmother. Jake was pacing the kitchen pounding his head with his fist; the boy readied himself, watching in trepidation. After what seemed an intolerably long time, his Father stopped and faced him, a low throaty growl erupted in the form of words, "When are you going to stop walking around with blinkers on. It's time you got off your high and mighty horse and started seeing things in perspective. I LOVE Cassie, I LOVE being married to her, and I most certainly LOVE the idea of having another child with her. Why do you persist in making life difficult for us all? If only you'd lighten up and give her a chance, this family could be so damned happy."

Dane stood arching his foot back and forth, "I don't know what you're talking about Dad."

Jake's eyes were pools of fury, "Cut the crap, you know exactly what I'm talking about. Your Mother just phoned. It seems someone told her I was tricked into fathering this baby. Any idea who could have told her that little bit of bullshit?" The boy pulled himself to his full height which wasn't far under his Father, and right now he felt his own fury raging within, "Dad, you're thirty nine now, too old to be having anymore kids. I just assumed she must have tricked you somehow."

"For crying out loud, my age is none of your damn business! Anyway this little incident is just the tip of the iceberg; you've been behaving like a proper little bastard for the last two years. I want to know what the real problem is!" He knew his son was on the verge of crying, yet his young stubborn pride withheld the force of nature, his lips were a tight line, "Speak to me Dane, tell me why you despise Cassie so much you won't even give her a chance."

Nature won out, glistening beads began to spill over his cheeks, "I DID! I did give her a chance, on your wedding day. And what did I get in return, a slap in the face for something I didn't do."

Jake was perplexed, surely that couldn't be the only reason for Dane's disagreeable attitude. He stared at the boy blankly, refusing to believe he could be that shallow to allow her one and only mistake taint his opinion for the rest of his life. No absolutely not, he shook his head, there had to be more to it than that. "Well Dane, judging by your track record, you could hardly have blamed her for automatically assuming you put the idea into Carly's head. And, let's not forget, I gave you the opportunity to explain, which you chose to ignore.

"See! *I KNEW* you'd take her side, you always take her side. Ever since *SHE* came on the scene, we take the back seat. *I HATE HER!!*" He ran from the room sobbing uncontrollably. Jake turned to the sink slamming his fist into it. *Damn!* What a mess. Dane was acting like an 8 year old, a spoilt brat. The very idea that he would think that he and the others came second to Cassie was preposterous. Obviously, the other children didn't feel that way. They had grown to accept her, so why the hell couldn't he. Jake grabbed a beer from the refrigerator and returned to his chair in front of the television. Cassie was right;

there was no point in trying to talk to Dane, he had made up his mind, and that was that. At that moment, she walked through the front foot. There were no parcels in her arm, yet the smile across her face was enigmatic. Jake smiled within at her sense of timing. Five minutes earlier and she would have witnessed his confrontation with Dane, and considering the way she had been feeling lately, it was something she could do without. He would tell her of course, but not yet, not until she was feeling more herself. "Well now; what's this, no mountain of parcels? Or are there that many you're having them delivered?"

"Don't be ridiculous. As a matter of fact, we didn't even reach the store. Philyce went into labour; well actually she'd been having pains all morning so technically we shouldn't have even gone; but anyway I ended up taking her to hospital, and that's where I've been."

His eyes traced her lips; they were moving nine to the dozen "Slow down will you. No tell me what you just said in English." Punching in playfully in the ribs, she laughed, "She had a girl, 7lb 5oz. And by the way it is Don's birthday on June 14th and we've been invited for dinner, so don't let me forget. Anything been happening around here?" Jake shook his head casually "No; not a darn thing. Want to order in a couple of pizzas for dinner." Her stomach turned at the thought, "You lot can have pizza, I'll have poached eggs."

Chapter 11

Catherine Rose was ten weeks old. They pulled up in front of Philyce and Don's two storey Spanish style home. Carly and Felicity gasped in awe, "Wow, they live in a palace." Cassie had been here numerous times, and although upon her initial visit, had been aptly impressed, and now took it all for granted. She smiled at their remark, "Not quite, although the way Aunty Phil has it furnished, it certainly could be fit for a Queen, so I want you all to promise me you won't touch anything unless you have been given permission." While the others were accenting, Dane felt physically sick, Aunty Phil! What crap! She was NOT his Aunty, and there was no way he'd call her that.

"Why did I have to come Dad? There was a good movie on tonight and I wanted to watch it."

"I'm sure you'll be allowed to watch it here Dane," Cassie answered. However, as though her voice was nothing more than the hum of an annoying mosquito, he completely ignored her.

"Dad, can I walk home, it's not far from here?"

Cassie tried again, "Dane I just said …" The boy looked at her, his eyes were like slithers of glass, "I'm speaking to my *FATHER!*" At that moment she realized with intimate agony, his contempt for her far exceeded a boyish grudge. There was no room for compromise as far as was concerned. She simply did not exist. Jake's reply was blunt, *"NO!"* He made no attempt to chastise his son for his rudeness. It was obvious he was following her previous advice, by deciding the best way to handle it was simply, not handle it at all.

Philyce was waiting for them on the verandah. Arched pylons made an impressive portico around the house. She led them through double doors into a wide foyer, where Don waited, his hand outstretched in welcome. He automatically wrapped one arm around Jake's shoulder, accepted his gift, a bottle of brandy with the other; and directed him through to his study where a large array of books adorned every wall. The girls looked around them in awe, their eyes like saucers, absorbed every detail. They looked up at Philyce; Carly almost had the inclination to curtsy. Dressed in an off the shoulder blue sequenced dress, she looked very much like a Princess, the only thing missing was the tiara.

Jeffrey as the first to speak; *"Wow!* I bet this house cost millions!" Cassie spun around with embarrassment, *"Jeff!"* Phil smiled and waved his comment away with her hand, "It's alright Cass, in his small eyes anything larger than a kennel is probably like a castle. Cassie had to bite her tongue. Was this woman implying they lived in a kennel? Philyce pinched Jeff's cheeks. "Not quite honey, but thanks for the compliment." He scowled deeply; he did not like his cheeks being pinched like a baby, and he certainly did know the difference. She laughed at his expression, "Would you like to see upstairs?" The frown was erased as his mouth curved into a broad grin, *"Wow! Yes please!"*

"O.K. follow me troops, but you must be very quiet because Catherine is asleep." She led them to the end of the foyer and turned right, where a wide carpeted stair case ascended to the second floor. Dane followed reluctantly. Even though he was suitably impressed, he was not about to show it. They entered the master bedroom where all four gasped,

Cassie laughed. The king size water bed stood proudly on thick plush carpet. Everything was white except for royal blue velvet curtains enhancing the French doors leading to the balcony, and the satin bedspread in the same colour. The walk through wardrobe was almost the size of a small bedroom, and passed the en-suite, which Cassie considered was almost the same size of their living room. A marble bath lay adjunct to the shower recess, which had double taps on each end, allowing two people to shower separately. Felicity pointed to a step "What's that up there?"

Philyce was starting to feel a little foppish, "A spa bath," she answered with pride. "A what?" the child echoed.

"It's a bath you sit in and bubbles squirt up at you, stupid," Jeffrey informed. Both women laughed, "Come on, I'll show you the TV room," Phil pointed to a door on the left, which took them back into the corridor. This room was pink; leather chairs surrounded the television and video system. The carpet was a light chocolate pure wool Berber. "Can we watch the television?" Dane enquired his voice just above a whisper.

"Sure you can, but we'll have dinner first," Phil replied.

With the tour complete, Carly noticed another door opposite the master bedroom, "What's in there?"

"That's the nursery, where Catherine is sleeping. There's a smaller bathroom adjoining that, and another four bedrooms and bathroom downstairs." It was obvious her initial attitude of 'I live in a big house, so what' had changed. Philyce was now out and out boasting, and Cassie felt the slightest hint of annoyance, or was it jealousy. She attempted to mask her feelings with a little sarcasm, "Gee, I'd certainly hate to have to clean this house, or do you employ a maid?" Phil ignored that remark; she cleared her throat, "Shall we go," and walked off leaving Cassie to follow. She was already a third the way down when Cassie approached the stairs. Don's voice, clearly audible drifted up to them. He was bragging about some sort of trophies he had. She was standing at the edge about to make her descent. Someone was behind her. She could feel warm breath on her neck. Whoever it was awfully close, too close. Within a split second the world began to turn. She instinctively reached out for the banister, but she was too close to the centre, her flaying hand grasped at nothing. A woman screamed, but she had almost reached Philyce before she realized it was her own terrifying scream reverberating with piercing urgency. Her friend cried out and lunged sideways trying to break her fall, but Cassie was moving too fast. Philyce felt her legs give way from the force of the impact, and she also began to fall.

Jake was running. He reached the two women just as they hit the bottom, Philyce landing on top of Cassie. His heart was hitting his ribs as he gently lifted Phil, who was stunned but seemed to be alright. She covered her mouth with her hand and gasped at the sight of her friend on the floor *"Oh my God, Cassie!"*

Cassie moaned, her body was racked with pain. She could smell blood, what blood, whose blood? An intense cramp gripped her abdomen, she screamed, *"JAKE!! THE BABY!! THE BABY'S COMING!!*

Don stared; panic seemed to have cemented his feet to the floor. Jake reached out and grabbed his leg, *"Shit man, don't just stand there; call the fucking ambulance!!"*

Jake paced nervously outside the delivery room. He hadn't been allowed in with her, and her occasional screams from behind the wide door was turning him into a man possessed.

"WHAT'S HAPPENING IN THERE!" he bellowed. His loud voice carrying down the silent corridor soon brought a nurse to reproach him. "Will you please keep your voice down Mr. Marshall?"

"Well shit lady, I'm not allowed in there and I want to know what the fuck is going on, that's my *WIFE AND CHILD!!"*

he combed his fingers through his hair, his ashen face creased with helplessness, eyes glistening with un spilt tears.

The stony faced nurse showed no compassion, "Here, here, please control your language or you'll have to wait outside the building. I'm sure your wife is receiving the best possible care, now *PLEASE* try and remain calm.

"Push Cassie, push hard!"

Her mind was a maze. Who was saying that? Who was the idiot telling her to push her baby into the world? Didn't he know it was too soon, that she still had twenty weeks to go? There was someone tall, dressed in white, but she couldn't make out his face, everything was blurred. His hands were covered with blood. Was that her blood? "Mrs. Marshall, we need your help, please you must push!"

"*NO!* My baby can't be born yet, it's too early!" she screamed again as another burning pain seared through her abdomen. Jake couldn't stand it any longer. He burst into the room, but was immediately restrained by two midwives. "I'm sorry Mr. Marshall; you'll have to wait outside." Thrashing his arms wildly, he broke free, *"Like fucking hell!"*

The Doctor spun around, "Let him stay, he may be able to help." Jake straightened his shoulders, "It's about bloody time."

Ignoring his choice of English, the grey haired man appealed to him, "Mr. Marshall, please, tell you wife she MUST help us."

Jake looked surprised; "I don't understand. You're supposed to be stopping the birth. Can't you give her needles or something to stop the contractions?"

The ageing Doctor was growing impatient and tried to control his temper between clenched teeth, "There is no time to argue; this child is crowning, but your wife is fighting against the contractions, and, if we don't get the baby born and the bleeding stopped, you could lose BOTH of them. It's as simple as that!"

Jake swallowed, he felt as though he had been hit by a Mac Truck. Moving to his wife's side, he spoke softly, tenderly, "Cass, honey, please do what the Doctor says."

She was crying steadily, her eyes were like glass, staring, unseeing; "But, Jake, he wants me to push our baby into this world and it's too soon."

"I know darling, but there's nothing they can do to stop him from being born, so you must help," she looked at him with helpless yearning. He tried to soothe her like a child by stroking her hair, "Please baby, please."

He choked back a sob as she responded to his pleading. The Doctor gestured his thanks with a nod. Jake turned away; the pain in her eyes was more overpowering than the physical torment enveloping her body. Without being asked, he left the room and cried openly in the corridor.

Forty five minutes later, the pale and lined face of the obstetrician emerged from behind the doors. It was obvious from his expression all was not well. Jake felt paralyzed, he wanted to speak but no words would come. He simply stared, trying to read the creased and somber face. "Mr. Marshall, I'm afraid your wife is gravely ill and I need your permission to perform a hysterectomy." The room began to spin, while Jake tried to comprehend what he was saying, "*NO! Absolutely not! I FORBID IT!*"

"I realise how hard this is for you Mr. Marshall, but there is simply no option. We can't stop the hemorrhaging, and unless we do this, she will most certainly die." Jake knitted his fingers behind his head and looked towards the ceiling, "It will kill her." He faced the Doctor again, "Are you sure there is no other way?" The elderly man placed a sympathetic hand on his shoulder and shook his head. He turned to leave, when Jake called him back, "What about the baby?"

"You have a son. He's in a humidity-crib and as about as well as could be expected under the circumstances. However, I'm sure you are well aware of the implications involved in a case like this. I'm sorry I can't give you any optimistic news. I don't know what your religious belief is Mr. Marshall, but perhaps now would be a good time to pray."

Chapter 12

Jake was sitting outside Cassies' private room, when Philyce arrived the next afternoon. He was staring into space, his unshaven face weary from no sleep. "Hello Jake, how is she?"

For a moment he said nothing, then he glanced up at her, his eyes appeared milky, "I don't know; I haven't been in yet."

Her surprise was obvious, "Why ever not?"

"She um," his voice trembled, "She had to have a hysterectomy, and I um; I just don't know what to say to her."

Philyce covered her face with her hands, "Oh dear God, no. And the baby, did it.."

"Die? No. Not yet at least, but the Doctor doesn't give us much hope. They're doing everything they can of course, but, I'm afraid our little boy will …" He couldn't go any further; his voice was gone, eyes spilling tears down his cheeks and neck. Phil hesitated unsure what to do; then she sat next to him and put her arm around him, he turned to her and sobbed; and she began to cry softly.

After several minutes he pulled back, wiping his nose and cheeks with the back of his hand. "Thank you Philyce, I just don't know what to do, I feel so helpless; useless; Cassie is in so much pain both physically and mentally and I can't do a thing to help her." A thought suddenly occurred; "I don't even know where my children are."

Clasping his arm gently, she smiled; "Don't worry Jake, they're fine. They stayed with us last night, and Skye came and took them to her place this morning. She asked me to tell you she'll have them for as long as necessary."

"Ok thanks" he responded. It was an automatic reply and Phil guessed at that precise moment, he didn't really care. "Are you going in now, or shall I go in first," she asked after they'd spent a moment in silence.

"What? Oh; it's ok you can go in, I still have to collect my thoughts," he waved his hand in dismissal, then casually rested his elbows on his knees, locked fingers and lowered his head bracing his forehead with knitted fists.

Philyce knocked several times, before a small voice finally beckoned entry. Cassie sat propped against the pillows like a cadaver, her face a bloodless mask, while her raven hair fell across the stark white linen like a winding sheet. Her eyes were pools of liquid staring helplessly at the ceiling. "Have you seen Jake?" she asked without turning.

Moving slowly to the bed, Phil felt physically shaken by the expression on her friend's pathetic face. What the hell does one say in an instance like this? She wanted to be light hearted and happy, however her words came out flat and full of pity. "He's right outside your door. Been there all night I'd say by the look of him. He'll be in later." Cassie didn't hear; "He's going to die Phil, my little boy is going to die, and there's not a damn thing I can do about it."

Phil removed a brush from her bag, and started gently stroking her friends' hair, "Don't give up hope honey. He *IS* hanging in; and where there is life there is always hope."

Cassie spun her head around, "*Hope you say!* That word doesn't exist. Not only is my baby going to die, there is absolutely no way I can ever *HOPE* to have any more children, thanks to that bastard outside that is too gutless to face me!"

"Cassie, honey, you can't possibly blame Jake for what's happened. It wasn't his fault you fell down the stairs."

"FELL!!! Fell my sisters' backside. I was *PUSHED!!!*

The blood descended rapidly to her friends' feet, she felt dizzy. A nauseas lump crept into her throat, "What are you saying Cass?"

Black clouds crossed the sun, blocking out the welcome warmth of the dark winters day. Grayness enveloped the room, casting eerie shadows across Cassies' face. She looked different, as she spoke her voice had changed to a low husky drawl, "What's the matter Phil, can't you understand English? I said I was *PUSHED!* I'm quite certain you know what that word means!"

The shocked woman inhaled sharply; this accusation was abominable. "But who would do such a thing. There were only us and the children upstairs?" Vacant slits of knowing stared back at her. Philyce felt scared, very scared, she shuddered involuntarily. Cassie was penetrating her with the eyes of woman possessed, an evil presence seemed to radiate from her soul and Phil felt panic rise in her throat like bile. "You think one of Jakes' kids pushed you?!"

Abnormal curls twisted her friends' mouth, a silent form of response that gripped Phils' stomach with horrific fear. But fear of what! Then as though the demon had suddenly been laid to rest, the narrow slits widened, revealing lucid well of sapphires. The terrified woman gasped, what the hell was she witnessing here? Cassie reached out and grabbed her hand with a touch so forceful, she wanted to recoil, but Cassies' steel grip was so intense, so powerful she couldn't budge. While her own face drained of color; Cassies' blossomed, almost as though she was draining all her friend's life giving energy into her own body. "Sing me a lullaby Phil, please."

For reasons unknown Philyce felt she couldn't question this odd request, instead she began to sing 'Rock a bye Baby' softly. Cassies' pupils began to dilate, she could see her reflection captured in the great black lakes, and for a split second she felt as though she was looking into the eyes of a blind woman, no, it was something worse, into the windows of the damned. Cassie released her hand, breaking the spell, then lay back against the pillows in an instant sleep. Phil stood, her legs liquefied, refusing to move for a moment. When she finally emerged from the room, Jake took one look at her completely shattered form, and sat bolt upright, "What the hell happened in there!?"

Shaking her head slowly, she reached out to him for support, "I don't know Jake. But I'll tell you this much, don't wait too long to see her, because if I didn't know better, I'd swear I've just been staring into the eyes of a woman regressing into the realm of the insane!" Deep craters creased his forehead, while his eyebrows merged above his nose. His mouth was open, but no sound came forth; she kissed him lightly on the cheek, then left, still shaking her head. He gazed after her until she had disappeared from view, that word filling his head like a migraine. *Insane!* She had said Cassie was drifting into insanity. Never! It just couldn't be, not Cassie; she was always so level headed, composed. Yes she was *ALWAYS* composed, well; all except that one time on their wedding day, but even then she managed to maintain composure after a brief time.

Inching his way slowly across the corridor, he pushed her door and peered in, she was asleep. One step further into the room and he could see her faced framed softly by silken tresses. She looked so peaceful and so damned lovely. Even in sleep her perfect mouth was curved in a faint smile. He glanced over the bare room, it was depressing, colorless. Flowers, that's what it needed. He would bring flowers, lots of them. It was when he turned to leave he felt something; some kind of magnetic force impelling him to face her again. Unblinking darkness stared at him. "Going so soon?" Unexplained fear washed through his veins, he forced a smile trying to erase the feeling of dread, "I thought you were asleep, and you looked so peaceful I didn't want to disturb you."

"How considerate you are!" The sarcasm was obvious, "Too bad you weren't that considerate when you gave that poor excuse of a Doctor the authority to take away my rights as a woman."

Jake felt his heart miss a beat, he moved to her side and picked up her hand, however she immediately wrenched free of his grasp as though his touch was acid. "Cassie; honey, I had no choice, you would have died otherwise."

Suddenly he felt as though he was witnessing a 'possession'. The complete change in her features was horrifying, and at that moment he realized exactly what Philyce had meant. Her mouth had become a tight line, she spoke with a voice not her own, "You son of a bitch! Don't you know what you've done? Death would have been a blessing compared to his living hell you're putting me through. I only married you because I knew you could give me what I wanted most, children. And now thanks to you and your fucking son, *MY* child is going to die and I *can NEVER, EVER have any more!!"* The pain in his eyes flashed like a neon sign, she smiled, "What's the matter Jake does the truth hurt? Does it hurt as much as I'm hurting? Is your blood boiling, and is the pain in your gut intensifying to the point of explosion!" She grabbed his shirt with the strength of ten men, "Do you feel as though you are dying inside. *Do you Jake! Do you*!" Their eyes were locked; his held back scalding tears, hers filled with hatred. Finally she released him with such force, he fell back, and her voice dropped to just above a whisper, "Because Jake, that's exactly how I feel."

Jake bit his bottom lip, he felt numb. She may as well have pushed a knife through his heart. Silence screamed at him, he wanted to leave, yet he understood her torment. They were just words; she didn't mean any of it. Besides she had every right to be angry, and if she needed to disgorge all her hatred and bitterness, why shouldn't it be at him, after all, he was the one closest to her. Now was not the time to crumble, he had to be strong, he had to be optimistic. "Honey, we can't give up yet, there could still be hope …" He stopped mid sentence when he saw her expression changing again, she covered her face with her hands, and then dragged them slowly down her cheeks leaving ugly red blotches embedded in her skin. She spoke softly, almost inaudibly; he had to strain to hear; "If I hear that word *HOPE* again, I shall scream." When she closed her eyes and moulded her head back against the pillows, he assumed she was going to sleep. He motioned to go, but she reached out for him with such unexpected speed, he froze with shock. "You really don't understand do you Jake. Our son is twenty weeks premature, his lungs aren't even developed properly yet. His only hop of survival is in my womb, which he has been deprived of. Not only is he fighting against the odds of nature, he is fighting God," she opened her eyes and with one last breath sighed; "And Jake, nobody wins against God."

Was it imagination or did the room suddenly become very cold. Her eyes were closed again, and her slow rhythmic breathing indicated she was asleep. Blowing into his hands and rubbing them together, he tried to bring back some form of warmth into his icy limbs. There was a coffee machine in the corridor that would warm him up and give him time to think.

Babies cried hungrily in the nursery as Jake sipped the steaming black brew in front of the glass windows. His baby wasn't amongst them, for he lay in the special nursery, in a humidity crib with hideous tubes and monitors attached to every part of his tiny body.

The formidable Doctor was approaching, his face was blank but his eyes said it all. At that moment Jake knew it was over. The waiting; the anguish had ended; their son had lost the battle of life.

Cassie touched the small coffin softly; her eyes were dry, her face reflecting nothing. Jake watched in silence. She would not speak of the accident, nor had there been any further referral to their conversation that day in the hospital. When he had joined the Doctor in her room to tell her the sad news, she had simply stated without emotion, "I want to name him Nathan, and I want a private funeral, no-one is to share that time with us, it is for us alone." So here they stood two weeks since their son's death, burying his tiny body in an isolated plot far away from the others; just the Minister, Cassie and himself. It was awful and her complete composure made him feel sick. It wasn't right, the entire situation was like a long bloody nightmare; he wanted to wake up; to run as far away from this miserable scene as possible.

Chapter 13

The warm breath of summer kissed gently across Jake's face as he sat atop his small plough. He watched Cassie in the distance hanging out the washing. It was too much for him. She had gone about the last five months as though nothing had happened; as if that terrible ordeal hadn't occurred. It wasn't right; she should have had a grieving period. "Maybe it is still to come," Phil had warned. For that reason Jake denied her request to find a job. If Phil was right and Cassie was sitting on a time bomb, then surely the first infant or even the first child named Nathan to come into her presence would detonate it, and, this was the reason he was certain, why Phil kept Catherine away from her. Although he couldn't keep her under lock and key, he couldn't risk a break down in a public place either, so, he offered her the job of doing his books and managing the accounts side of things while he sowed and reaped. It was working out rather well, and when she hit on the idea of selling the sub-standard vegetables at a cheaper rate from their home, instead of giving them away, they had begun to show a marked profit increase of twenty per cent.

Yet it wasn't enough. She needed something else, he sensed it. A different concept to keep her mind alert on the days she had free. Perhaps Don held the answer. He had mentioned he needed someone part time to type up his contracts and manage the books. Philyce had done it all before the baby arrived, but now she was far too busy and everything was falling behind. Of course the only problem was Don worked from home, so it meant her going back into that house; but surely after all this time, if she was going to break down and crumble it would have happened by now.

Cassie sat at the kitchen table, Jakes' ledgers before her. She had seen him watching her from afar and she knew what he was thinking. What they ALL were thinking. They were waiting for her to shatter into a million pieces. She closed her eyes against the vision of her tiny infant lying so cold and still in the coffin. None of them knew her pain. They didn't understand that even if she lived to be one hundred, it wouldn't be long enough to shed the tears lying dormant inside her.

Even her best friend had tried to entice her into talking about it, to let go and cry. But how could she explain her heart was not filled with grief. It was anger encompassing her soul, a blind rage that would be appeased when justice was done. Only then would this living nightmare be over. Only then would her dead baby rest in peace; and what of Jake? Had he not given permission for them to cut into her and remove her womb, in turn denying all her unborn children the right of conception? After all, he had already helped give life to four so why should he care. She shook her head slowly; he must pay for his crime also. Somehow she would find a way to make him pay.

It was late before Jake came in. All except Cassie were in bed. She removed his dinner from the oven and placed it in front of him. Then without a word, turned and started for the bedroom. Jake pushed the chair back and stood abruptly, grabbing her arm, "Cass, don't go to bed, not yet. We haven't made love since …" he hesitated, "since before everything happened, and I want you tonight. She looked into his pleading

Kerry Christine Vrossink

eyes with sapphires of ice. Jake tightened his grip, "Damn it Cassie, I need you. Don't make me beg!"

"I'm not ready Jake," she replied softly. He released her and slowly began caressing her shoulders, deliberately sliding the fine straps of her night dress down. He felt her body grow rigid beneath his trembling fingers, "I told you I'm not ready." Catching his breath sharply, he spun her around to face him fully.

"Can you at least tell me, when the hell you will be?!"

As far as she was concerned, she no longer needed his seed within her, she would never be ready. Her defiant lips parted slightly as she whispered; "No."

During the weeks that followed, Jake worked later and later into the night, until finally it was the early hours of the morning before he retired. Cassie no longer kept his dinner warm since he had also stopped eating the evening meal. She knew he wasn't really working, that he was simply finding things to do in the packing shed, but she didn't care. He was leaving her alone and that's what mattered.

It wasn't until Christmas Day, when Jake retreated back to work straight after lunch; the children noticed something was amiss between them.

Jeffrey couldn't understand this unusual behavior and commented, "How come Dad's working today? He never works Christmas Day, *NEVER*."

Cassie eyed him speculatively, "Well, he has a new contract with a cannery, so I guess he wants to keep on top of everything," she commenced clearing the table, a gesture which usually indicated the closure of the subject.

Carly was too interested in her present to worry about what her Father was doing or why; "Can I please leave the table and try out my new roller skates?"

Her stepmother shrugged, "I suppose so. But don't get

dirty. Your Mother will be here shortly to take you to your Grandparent's house."

Dane intervened, "Dad said she couldn't use them until he was there to supervise."

Cassie was growing impatient. It was frightfully hot and she couldn't be bothered with small talk or debates; "Oh for goodness sake, stop being an old woman. Your Father probably won't get around to it for weeks. It was stupid of him to buy something she can't enjoy unless he's around," she nodded at the child, still waiting for a direct answer, "Go on, off you go. Just be careful."

When Rae arrived, Cassie had cleaned up and applied a little make-up. Her denim shorts accentuated her long slender legs, while the off the shoulder top, enhanced the slim line of her neck and back. She looked good and she knew it. Not that she really gave a damn what this woman thought of her, but this would be the first time they had made eye contact and she wanted to be seen at her best not worst.

The two women glanced over each other casually, no introductions were necessary and no polite formalities taken.

"Where's Jake?" Rae asked.

"Working"

"Really; that's unusual."

Cassie didn't feel inclined to get into this conversation with her, she smiled and pointed to the corridor, "All their bags are packed. When will you be bringing them home?"

Rae's face softened as Carly came running into her arms. Bending down she embraced the child with an enormous hug, "New Year's Day. Hello darling. What have you got there?"

"Roller skates. Santa brought them. Aren't they neat?" her daughter answered proudly.

"Yes darling, they're lovely," but when Carly had disappeared outside, Rae's face creased with rage; "rather a stupid present to give a child that age, don't you think!? What if she falls and breaks her leg or something!?"

Cassie shrugged, "You'll have to take that up with Jake. They were his idea, not mine."

They stared at each other in silence for a full minute before Dane came in, breaking the air of contempt. "Hi Mum!" She turned, the corners of her mouth curled slightly, "Hi yourself." Cassie noticed a moment of uncertainty between them. Even when they embraced it seemed forced. He cleared his throat, "Do you mind if I don't come with you Mum?"

Rae looked surprised, "Well no, but why?" Cassie was listening with great interest. His remark had taken her by surprise also and his reason, she was sure, would have to be a good one. Although Rae and Dane were obviously awkward in each others' company, Cassie guessed the idea that Dane would choose to stay with his Father, rather than the opportunity of a week with her, inconceivable, and very much out of the question.

"Well it's just that I got a computer for Christmas, and, I um, would really like to hang around here and play around with it."

"Oh I see," she glanced at Cassie who was eyeing her with amusement. "Very well, I'll bring your gifts back when I bring the others home." Within ten minutes Rae had gathered the other three and left.

Rae paced nervously on the verandah of her parents large Tudor style home. She had toyed with her food during dinner and now while the children played happily with their presents, she couldn't settle. Moya Barrett watched her daughter through the wire screen door, she had never seen Rae so uneasy and it worried her. Carl stood beside his wife encircling her slim waist with his arm. He had been a very content man since he had convinced Rae to bring his Grandchildren and stay with them for a week, but now he observed her odd behavior with a hint of concern also. Kissing his wife softly on the cheek, whispered, "What do you suppose is worrying her?"

The slightly built woman who was simply an older version of her daughter, shook her head, "I don't know, but I think I had better find out." The door seemed to groan in protest as she opened it, Rae turned and faced her Mother with a solemn look. Moya smiled and embraced her with a comforting hug, "What's the matter honey, you seem on edge?"

For the past thirty minutes Rae had been debating whether or not to mention her uneasy feelings to her parents, now the decision had been made simple, "It's that woman."

"What woman?"

"Jake's wife, Cassie," she sighed deeply; "There's something about her Mum, I can't quite put my finger on it, but there's something terribly wrong."

"Oh sweetheart is that all. It's only natural you would feel strangely towards her," her Mother laughed, "After all she is married to your ex husband and a tiny bit of jealousy is to be expected."

Rae felt angry at being taken so lightly, "Jealousy has nothing to do with it. I don't give a damn that Jake re-married; it's *HER!* There's something about *HER.* If there's one thing I'm good at Mum, it's judging people and you know for a fact my first impressions are very rarely wrong." Her Mother had raised one eyebrow, "Rae I really think you are over reacting."

"Mother you weren't there, you didn't look into those eyes of, of absolutely nothing," she snapped, "And then there is Dane."

"What about Dane?"

Rae threw her arms in the air, "The way he was looking at her. She wasn't aware of it but I certainly was. There was lust written all over his face and I'm frightened to death!"

"But darling Dane despises her, he told me that himself."

A moment of silence lapsed, Rae lifted her eyes to the sky towards the Southern Cross. Her voice was edged with emotion as she spoke very softly, "Yes that's what I thought too, but believe me Mum things have obviously changed."

Cassie emerged from the bathroom wrapped only in a towel. Jake was still working, she laughed to herself as she thought of him sitting in the packing shed most likely reading a book or doing a crossword. Dropping the towel she stood in front of the mirror running her hands over the smooth contours of her naked body. Just lately she'd been having certain urges. Whenever she saw a handsome man at the supermarket or encountered any of Jake's well presented clients she felt a tightening in her loins and a quickening in her pulse. Yet as much as her body craved satisfaction Jake was not the one to do it. Slipping into her night dress, she thought of Don. The same look she had seen that day in the hospital had since appeared several times. And his kiss of welcome whenever they met seemed to linger more and more with each occasion.

"Are you and Dad having problems?" The voice came from behind, she spun around startled. "That's none of your damn business." He was inches from her, their eyes were level and the look on his face frightened her. She glanced at the door, it was closed. He must have been hiding in the walk-in robe. "How long have you been in my room?"

Dane raised his hand to her face, running it softly down her cheek and neck, allowing it to rest on her shoulder. His touch was clammy and his fingers trembled, "Long enough to see you caressing your body and fondle your breasts in front of the mirror. Long enough to know you are obviously yearning a man's touch."

Cassie pulled away horrified, but he reached out and grabbed her arms in a vice like grip. She stared into his sea colored eyes speechless for a moment before her body began to shake with uncontrollable laughter, "Oh my goodness Dane, you're not seriously trying to seduce me are you?"

His face contorted with anger, she was laughing at him. The bitch was actually laughing. "I've heard you arguing with Dad about sex. You haven't had any for months, but you and I both know how much you want a man."

Cassie wrenched free from his grasp, "Yes Dane, you are quite right. I haven't had any sex for months and I *DO* want a man: *A MAN* Dane, not a bloody *CHILD*. Do you know what a man is … someone with stubble around his chin, instead of bum fluff."

Those words cut through him like a knife. He lashed out and caught the side of her face with his hand, the force of which sent her reeling back onto the bed. She bit her lip from the intensity of the impact, blood trickled slowly down her chin while the stinging pain brought tears to her eyes, but again she laughed, "Go back to your smutty books Dane and carry on playing with yourself behind your bedroom door like you normally do."

The boy leered at her naked form through the sheer fabric of her night gown. His arousal was agonizing, yet his rage was building beyond control; picking up a vase from the dressing table he moved slowly toward her. She instinctively brought her arm across her face waiting for the blow.

"*DANE!*" Jakes voice ripped through the room like a thunder bolt. The vase fell to the floor shattering into hundreds of pieces. He turned to face his Father who was standing directly behind, and then he saw Jake's fist inches from his face. With one sweeping blow, he felt his jaw burning with pain; darkness encompassed the room as he crumbled to the ground. Jake lifted the heavy boy under his arms and dragged him to his room. When he returned Cassie was in the bathroom rinsing the blood from her mouth.

"Want to tell me what the hell was going on?" his voice was quivering.

She looked at him through the mirror, "Your son had the misconception I needed a man, and decided he was the one to do it."

Jake glanced over her attire briefly, "Little wonder if you parade around dressed like that in front of him." Her mind was a whirl, he was blaming her. He actually had the audacity to imply it was all her fault, she couldn't believe it. Without thinking, she swung around, her hand poised to strike his face, but he was ready and grabbed her wrist. "No, I think not." The seconds were passing, she could feel her hand throbbing from lack of blood, still he held her, secured in his steel grip with a strength she was unaware he had. When he finally released her roughly, her wrist was burning and her hand turning blue. "We'll discuss this in the morning," he stated; turned and left. When she entered the bedroom, his pillow and a blanket were missing, obviously he was sleeping elsewhere.

Jake lay on an old straw mattress in the shed with nothing around him except cardboard boxes. The mattress was dreadfully lumpy and he was far from comfortable, but he needed to be alone, he needed time to decide what the best action would be after witnessing that horrific scene. He had reacted badly but he couldn't help it, it had been instinctive. The sight that beheld him had nauseated him and even made him jealous. He was furious with his son for even contemplating the idea, yet he accused Cassie of what: teasing? She would never have led the boy on and he knew it, so why did he say such a stupid thing. Because now Dane was almost a man and he had seen her naked, the one thing he held sacred and he was jealous, plain and simple.

Sleep eluded him as he tossed and turned until the first grey streaks of dawn broke through the cracked and dusty window.

The table was set and breakfast cooking when Cassie ambled in. Her bottom lip was swollen and dried blood crusted in the corner of her mouth. She avoided eye contact when he handed her a cup of coffee. No words passed, she accepted it and pulled up a chair sitting with her back to him. He shook his head and moved around the table opposite her. "I've made a decision."

Cassie looked at him over the rim of her cup, "I'm going to send Dane to Carl and Moya. I'll simply say the two of you just can't get along, that should be a good enough explanation. I know Rae would only find excuses why she can't have him and if she objects to these arrangements," he sighed, "well it's just doo damn bad."

She felt panic rise in her throat. If Jake sent Dane away she would never see justice done. "You're making too much of this Jake. If you send him away like an unwanted puppy, he'll never forgive you and you'll lose him. What happened last night was a mistake. He sensed you and I were having a few problems and I guess his idea was to comfort me, as a man would. Nothing *happened* Jake; I think you should just forget it."

"*Forget it!*" He pushed his chair back abruptly, stood and began to pace until he was able to regain some composure, and then faced her again. "Cassie he was about to crown you with a crystal vase. How the hell am I supposed to forget it?"

"I'm to blame. I provoked him into such a rage; I don't even think he was aware of his actions." Jake studied her carefully, "How? In what way could you have brought him to the point of attempted murder?"

She held his gaze with unblinking eyes, "I laughed at him. He was doing his best to seduce me and I laughed at him. I told him I wanted a man not a child."

"Is that how you got your swollen lip?" She nodded and continued; "Even after he struck me I laughed. I told him to go back to playing with himself in his bedroom with his dirty books. That's when he grabbed the vase, and, well, you know the rest."

Dane lay on his bed, arms folded behind his head. He also had spent a sleepless night. His jaw was badly bruised and hurt like hell, not to mention the thunderous headache hammering away in his brain. He could hear their voices echoing from the kitchen, hers unclear, but his Father's loud and very distinct. He felt so damn stupid. In a moment of passion he thought he could seduce her. He tried to be as seductive and manly as he could, but she called him a child and laughed in his face. Boy was he a jerk. How the hell was he supposed to explain this one? Maybe he could lie and say he had been drinking. Yes, that was good. He would say he was drunk and didn't know what he was doing. But one thing was for sure, she would never laugh at him again, never.

As if on cue Jake knocked on his door, waited a moment and entered. Dane was staring at the ceiling. Positioning himself on Jeffrey's bed opposite, he sat in silence, waiting. Dane cleared his throat and spoke in a small voice, "I suppose you want some kind of explanation.

"That's what I'm here for."

The boy sat up and faced his Father, "I was drunk Dad. I had a bottle of vodka hidden in my drawer and I'd been drinking all afternoon. I walked past your room and saw Cassie standing in front of the mirror naked," he sighed in resignation, "I guess I just went crazy."

"I see; and where did you get the Vodka?"

"One of my mates got it for me" he lied.

Jake stood; staring at his son for what seemed an eternity. When Dane began to squirm uncomfortably under his intense gaze; he responded:

"Yes well, that may explain your advances, however, it

doesn't explain why you hit her, or why you were about to crack her skull open with the vase."

Dane lowered his eyes in shame. He was inadvertently folding and refolding the corner of his sheet with trembling hands. He felt so degraded he wanted to die. "She laughed at me."

Jake's mind reflected back twenty two years. He was seventeen and had the 'hots' for his science teacher, Miss Becker, the entire year. On the last day of school he had offered to stay behind and help her clean up, then when they had finished he decided to make his move. He had kissed her sloppily on the mouth as he attempted to touch her breast, and said something stupid like: "let's make love." Her reaction was embedded in his brain and would be forevermore. At first she had looked at him appalled, then she had burst out laughing and he remembered how foolish, embarrassed and angry he felt. Now as he looked at his son twisting and turning the sheet like a five year old, he felt a wave of compassion. "Alright Dane, we'll let it go this time, but if anything like this ever happens again, I'll have you charged and put away so fast, you won't see your feet for dust. Do I make myself clear?"

Dane looked up at his Father astounded. He hadn't expected to get off this light, "Sure, I understand."

"Good," he rose, "Now, get dressed and come into the kitchen. I think you owe Cassie an apology, don't you?"

He nodded, but after Jake had left he climbed back under the sheets, "Like hell," he muttered.

Chapter 14

The clock struck midnight sending everyone into the old rendition of Auld Lang Syne. Another year gone; another beginning. Jake prayed this year would be better than the last. It had to be; surely it couldn't be any worse; his thoughts were interrupted when he noticed Cassie sitting a little too closely to Don singing happily. Phylice had stayed home with a headache, she claimed, but Jake strongly suspected she wanted to keep Catherine away from her friend in case it triggered the fuse she was certain Cassie was sitting on.

Dane remained obscure all week and was even now in his room, but Jake didn't pressure him, he knew the boy was still ashamed and didn't want to have to make excuses for his yellowing bruise.

A hand on his shoulder brought him back to the present, "Happy New Year buddy," Roger was saying, "Yes, Happy New Year," he replied. His friend led him to a quiet corner away from the reveling guests, "Listen Jake I don't want to stick my nose where it's not wanted, but if I was you, I'd keep an eye on that little bloke Don. He seems a little too preoccupied with your wife in my opinion!"

Jake chuckled, "You're not serious."

"You may think it's funny old boy, but they've been head to head all night. I can't believe you haven't noticed."

"Roger, my old friend, don't be overly concerned. Don offered Cassie a part-time job, which is why I'm sure they have had their heads together most of the night," he gave Roger a pat on the back, "They're only discussing the details I'm sure."

Roger watched him walk away, "You bloody fool," he thought.

Rae drove the children home later that afternoon. Carly limped in behind Jeffrey, with grazed elbows and knees. Jake gave his ex wife an abrasive look, she retaliated verbally; "You're the one who gave her those stupid bloody roller skates. Honestly Jake, what were you thinking!?"

"She's growing up Rae. I can't keep her wrapped in cotton wool for the rest of her life," he answered casually.

Rae almost choked on her anger, "She's only seven! Still a baby; too bloody young to be given anything as dangerous as these!" With that she pushed the offensive items into his arms. "If you've got any brains at all, you'll hide them away for a few more years."

Jake bent down and lifted his daughter in his arms, "Maybe Mum is right Carly. Perhaps we should put them away until you are a little bit older." Her large helpless eyes were filling with tears, "But Daddy, you told me they were from Santa; why would he give me anything that was too old for me?"

The logic in her question left him temporarily speechless; he looked over at Rae, "Don't look at me for help. You can get yourself out of that one, I'm leaving."

Cassie had been sun baking out the back when she heard Rae's car pulling into the drive. She had entered through the laundry door in time to hear the end of the conversation. As much as she hated to admit it, she had to agree with Rae, however since she had refused to help Jake select the gifts, she had to go along with his choice without question. Little did she know that he had inadvertently chosen the present that would see the onset of her justice and that this year he would begin to pay for his transgression.

Jake awoke with a feeling of dread. It was the 3rd of February and he had to get the baby carrots to the cannery; but that wasn't anything out of the ordinary and could not explain the peculiar feeling shrouding over him. Even the day was eerie. Yesterday the sun beat down with full force, not even a wisp of a cloud could be seen for miles, yet this morning light rain descended steadily from grey clouds that appeared to blanket the entire sky and hindering the red glow of dawn trying desperately to break through over the horizon. By five o'clock he was driving slowly along the highway to the canning factory. His dented and rusty pick-up rattled and groaned in protest; it was very old and needed a lot of tender loving care. "Come on old girl," he coaxed as the rain intensified and windscreen wipers threatened to die.

The knot in his stomach tightened, there was something wrong. Everyone had still been asleep when he left, everything seemed normal; yet this knot, this feeling of dread remained.

Felicity knocked on the bedroom door, "Wake up Cassie. Today's the first day of school remember; you have to make our lunches." Opening one eye she groaned and rolled over to face the clock; it was seven thirty already, Jake had forgotten to re-set the alarm. "Ok, I'm awake. Make yourself some toast or something."

Dane decided he wasn't returning to school, and with neither Cassie nor Jake wanting an argument had simply agreed and left him to his own devices. She didn't know if he was still in bed or if he'd gone with Jake but frankly didn't care. And now with breakfast over she drove the children to school, saw them settled in their class rooms, then made her way to Don's office. In the weeks since she had started working for him, she had managed to bring all his outstanding contracts and book keeping up to date. Don was very pleased, but not half as pleased as she was with herself. He was sitting behind her desk reading the paper when she entered. "What a day!" he remarked, "Hot as hell and raining cats and dogs at the same time."

"I see Jake's ex father in law finally caught the bastard murdering those young girls!" he continued.

Cassie nodded, "Yes, just because he felt like it, I believe. Makes you wonder what sort of monsters could conceive demons like that!"

He raised his eyebrows at her strange remark and peered at her over the rim of his glasses, "Indeed!" and changed the subject "So tell me, did you get the kids all settled in school?" She nodded, "All except Dane. He has decided not to finish his last year and is supposedly working with Jake until he finds something more suitable. But I didn't see him this morning so I don't know whether he actually went with Jake or not, frankly I don't really care." She sighed; "personally I think he's destined to be a no hoper; he has no qualifications for anything and I really don't think he'll stay with Jake for long."

Don laughed, "Some of my richest clients started that way. Then all of a sudden they venture onto some scheme and away they go, all the way to the bank!"

"Perhaps, but I'm sure they were motivated towards some sort of goal. Dane just seems to plod along, one day at a time with nothing in particular urging him on."

Don rose and moved beside her. She felt her stomach tingle when he placed his hand on her shoulder and left it there. "What say I take you for lunch somewhere today? Since you've been so efficient; there isn't much to do; only a bit of filing, so, what do you think; a counter lunch at the tavern?"

"Sure, that would be very nice."

Jake drove his old jalopy into the garage next to the packing shed. There was no sign of Dane. He could see one of the work hands tilling the soil to the far north, and another picking lettuce from the main crop, but … *NO* Dane! He sighed, he had known it would be touch and go giving Dane a Job, but he did expect him to turn up for the *FIRST* day at least! He slammed the drivers' door and stormed off into the house and into his room; where he lay still comfortably asleep. Jake was livid, he yanked the boy, mattress and all onto the floor. Dane sat up with start, "*What the..!*"

His Father roared, "*Get up!* You're supposed to be helping David pick the lettuce!"

Dane scratched his head, "Sorry, guess I slept in."

"*Slept in!* It's one o'clock in the bloody afternoon. You've been asleep most of the bloody day. Now get to, and if this happens again, you can go and join the unemployment line at the job Centre." Within five minutes, Dane was dressed and heading in the general direction of the lettuce crops. Jake shook his head, Cassie had told him employing Dane wasn't a very good idea. She warned him, the boy would take advantage and abuse the situation. But no, he had to give his son a chance; he had to prove her wrong. Ever since the incident they no longer speak of, Jake had been determined to prove Dane a responsible human being. Seems he was wrong again.

Don watched intently as Cassie ate her dessert. She was unlike any other woman he had ever come across in his life. Strong willed, determined and lovely. These were wonderful attributes in a female. He loved Philyce, but she was soft and helpless, so typically feminine it was boring. Cassie was a real treat, a real challenge. She caught him eyeing her and smiled; Is something wrong. Have I got spinach in my teeth or something?" He laughed, then grew serious, "How are you Cassie? I mean really."

Her look was of surprise, "I'm fine. Why do you ask?"

"Well, I know it's none of my business, but, both Phil and I have noticed things seemed to have changed between you and Jake since ..."

Since Nathan died. You don't have to be afraid to say it. Yes I suppose they have. These days he seems more of an employer than a husband. But, really Don, please don't worry, we'll work things out eventually." She patted the corners of her mouth with a napkin. "Well, shall we go?"

They left the tavern, but Don turned West instead of continuing straight along the highway. "Where are we going?" she asked surprised.

"It's such a lovely day; I thought we might drive down to the beach."

She burst into laughter, "Are you serious? It hasn't stopped raining!"

"There is no better time to watch the ocean, than when it is re-grouping the water the sun so mercilessly stole. Then watch it reach out angrily, twisting and turning, daring anyone to ride its unforgiving waves. He looked at her, she shuddered and wanted to say 'I think you are a fruit loop' but instead nodded her head "since you put it that way, I guess it is a nice day after all!"

A few surfers bravely defied the waves trying desperately to remain in control, and after crashing into the swell regained their boards and declined a second round, leaving them alone in the car park.

"Isn't it fabulous?!" Don called out like an excited child. Cassie couldn't see anything fabulous about the sea on a wet and windy day, but agreed just the same. Her heart missed a beat when she noticed Don looking at her with a certain glint in his eye that she once thought she had imagined. At that moment it became obviously clear why he had brought her here. When he reached across and touched her face softly, the urge she had been repressing all these months re-surfaced. His hand slid from her cheek down to her breast, his eyes following hers with trepidation; he was waiting for a reaction, adverse or otherwise. When none ensued, he grew bolder and pulled her across into his arms kissing her lightly on the mouth. With a free hand, he inched it under skirt and along her thigh. It was more than Cassie could stand, her juices began to flow and she felt herself involuntarily rubbing her breasts against him, and voiced no comment when suddenly she was thrown back as the seat collapsed and he slowly slid her panties down. He was going to make love to her there and now. Guilt washed through her, but not for Jake, for Philyce. History was repeating itself. Only this time she was allowing her best friends husband seduce her, and just as she did before she lay back and let him bring her to a climax, without giving it another thought.

Jake drained his glass and poured another beer. His stomach was still doing somersaults and for the life of him, he couldn't figure out why. The last time he experienced anything as uneasy as this, was when he came in from work, and found Rae standing at the door with her suitcases. Perhaps Cassie was going to come home and tell him she was leaving. It certainly wouldn't come as surprise, after all that had happened in the last year; a part of him expected it.

The rain subsided just as she pulled into the drive. Carly and Felicity almost jumped from the car and ran in full of news about the first day school. But he wasn't listening, he was too busy searching Cassies' face for some sort of clue, but she was smiling and seemed happier than she had been for a long time. Carly realized her Father was preoccupied and she was speaking to deaf ears, and decided to take advantage of the situation. "Dad can I have my roller skates?"

He forgot he had forbidden her from using them until she was eight, "Yes, they're in my wardrobe … Cass sit down I want to talk to you."

Guilt crept into her eyes, her cheeks felt flushed and burning. He must know. His face was so straight, his mood so solemn, he must know. Silently she complied, and instantly began toying with invisible crumbs on the table. "Cass, did anything unusual happen today?" What was he up to? Was he going to play on her conscience until she confessed? Still picking at the table cloth she shook her head, "No."

"Will you look at me!?" Slowly she raised her eyes, "Thank you, I find it a little disconcerting speaking to the top of your head," he paused, "Did you have any near misses in the car, or are the kids in any trouble?" The corners of her mouth turned up slightly, he didn't know, there was something else on his mind, "No Jake. Why?"

Covering his face with his hands he sighed, "I don't know, I've had this really uneasy feeling all day, and it's really bugging me."

They both heard the screech of brakes and the loud thud. Cassie didn't take too much notice, after all it was a common occurrence living where they did to hear motorists hitting foxes or the odd kangaroo, but Jake had turned deathly pale, he started to retch and before they heard the first scream, he was running. He stumbled over the coffee table in his haste falling heavily, yet he was on his feet and out of the door before she could reach him.

Felicity was screaming. Jeffrey's bike was laying in the middle of the road with the boy a sobbing heap beside it. Cassie's first thought was that he had been hit by a car, but

Jake was running towards something else sprawled across the road about in the opposite direction.

When she reached him, he was laying across whatever it was, trembling uncontrollably. His words were incoherent; all she could make out was ambulance. With the greatest care, she secured his shoulders and lifted him to the side. Nausea instantly filled her mouth; she turned away and brought up her lunch. Carly was a blood soaked mass of flesh. Her head had a four inch dent in it and her face, arms and legs were void of skin, obviously from being dragged along the road. The skates had been ripped from her feet and every bone in her body appeared broken. Jake was screaming by now and begging Cassie to commence CPR. She gathered him in her arms and very softly stroked his hair, "Jake, honey, it's no use; she's gone. No-one can revive her. What I want you to do is wait here and divert any traffic while I ring the police and the ambulance. Do you think you can do that?" He nodded, but after she walked a couple of meters, she looked around to find him sitting next to his daughter, his eyes closed and his body jerking spasmodically.

Dane was approaching the end of the drive by the time she reached it, he looked confused, "I heard a loud bang and then all this screaming, what's going on?"

"Don't ask questions just do me a favor and ring the police and ambulance; *NOW!!!!!*" Dane turned and ran back to the house. She went back to Jake who was lying next to Carly sobbing. She looked both ways and noted there was NO car to be seen, whoever had done this wasn't hanging around.

By the time the police arrived, Carly had been placed in the back of the ambulance and the paramedics were attending to Jake. Jeffrey and Felicity were sitting on the verge, while Dane stood alone propped against a tree. Cassie was trying to remain calm, but seeing Jake in this condition together with her tainted conscience, seemed to be drawing strength from her legs, and, as the two policemen approached, she felt herself drop; a pair of burly arms reached out preventing a complete collapse. "Are you alright Madam?"

"Yes, thank you. My legs just seemed to liquefy for moment, but, they're alright now."

The young constable smiled, "Good. Can you tell me what happened?"

"Actually; no! My husband and I were in the house, when we heard a screech of brakes and then a thud. When we raced out, we found Carly on the road. But the two other children were outside, I haven't had a chance to question them yet, but I'm sure they must have seen something."

Jeffrey wiped the tears from his eyes, as the policeman crouched in front of him, "Hi there young fellow, how are you doing?"

He sniffed, "O.K. I guess."

"That's the boy," he coaxed, "Did you by any chance see what happened?" He nodded slowly. The young man pulled out a note book and waited, but the boy just stared. "Can you tell me?" he finally asked softly. He nodded again, and lowered his eyes to the ground, "I was riding home from school behind this big yellow car. I was just there," he pointed to where he had dropped his bike on the road, when all of a sudden I saw Carly come flying down the drive on her roller skates, straight onto the road. The car tried to stop, but it couldn't, and the next thing I saw was Carly caught underneath and being dragged down the road." He started to cry and the constable placed a gentle hand on his shoulder, "That's alright son, I know how hard this is for you. Can you just tell me if you know what sort of car it was and maybe the color?" Jeffrey thought for a moment, and then shook his head, "I just know it was bigger than a normal car; sort of long and it was yellow." Would you say it was an old car or a new one?" He shrugged, "I don't know."

Cassie interrupted, "I don't know if this is much help, but, one of the teachers at the high school drives a yellow station wagon. And, I believe he lives about four streets from here." The policeman stopped writing, "Would you happen to know his name?"

Tapping her forehead with her a finger, "Yes, let me think for a moment; John Yates; Yes that's his name I'm sure of it; he used to be Danes Science Teacher."

"Thank you Mrs. Marshall, we'll check it out straight away; oh and I'm very sorry about your daughter," the older constable said, but as they walked away whispered to his partner; "Some Mother, as calm as you please, not a tear in her eye, and a heart of stone."

Cassie hadn't bothered explaining she was a stepdaughter, she didn't care if she wasn't showing the 'right' emotion … how could she, she didn't feel anything, literally didn't feel any emotion at all. However, now came the hard part, someone had to ring Rae and since obviously Jake was in no condition to do it, that only left her or Dane. And, as much as she disliked Dane, it really wouldn't be fair to expect him to tell his Mother his sister had died, especially under the condition she died. No alas it would have to be her.

Chapter 15

Cassie stood back away from the rest who were amassed together like a clump of caterpillars. Jake had his arm entwined around Rae; she had her head buried deep into his shoulder. This was a far cry from the outburst of hysteria and accusations; she had spat forth a week ago. Cassie had tried to break the news as calmly and delicately as she could while Rae stood at the other end of the receiver in complete silence. "Are you still there?" she had to keep asking. It was only the fact she could hear Rae's stilted breathing, she knew she was. Then fifty minutes later while Jake sat on the chair, head in hands and rocking pathetically, Rae and Carl had burst in.

She had to smile when she thought of that horrific scene; instead of consoling each other the lay of blame was bounced back and forth like a tennis match. *"I TOLD YOU NOT TO BUY THOSE DAMN SKATES!!"* Rae had screamed; retaliated with Jake's pitiful response, "If you'd been a proper Mother and taken the children to live with you, none of this would have happened. *I DON'T KNOW WHAT TO BUY KIDS FOR CHRISTMAS!!"*

Then it was her turn for blame; *"WELL WHY DIDN'T YOUR WIFE* do the Christmas shopping if you're that incompetent!"* Their voices had come to fever pitch and if it hadn't been for Carl pacifying and soothing, Cassie was certain it would have physically come to blows. But now here they were comforting each other like perfect parents would.

Don and Philyce stood a little to her right, she could feel his eyes turning to her occasionally while his hand came out and squeezed hers gently; a gesture which wasn't required since she felt no grief or remorse. In fact, a strange stirring of excitement had filled her stomach since the accident. Her child had been indirectly taken by one of his children, now one of his had been taken also. It was retribution plain and simple.

Back at home after the funeral Jake went straight to the bedroom and slammed the door. He could be heard sobbing from the kitchen and every now and again he would shout *"IT SHOULD HAVE BEEN ME!!"* This procedure had been ongoing since Carly's death, and, at first she tried to console him, now she simply closed the door and left him to it.

Don and Philyce waited patiently in the kitchen unsure of what to say or do next. Phil shuffled uncomfortably in her chair. She hadn't wanted to come back but Don had insisted, "It's the right thing to do," he explained. Still she was uneasy and apprehensive. Things just weren't right; Cassie almost seemed happy and where everyone else had tears rolling down their cheeks at the cemetery; she had actually smiled slightly. Phil had avoided her friend as best she could after their conversation in the hospital, no longer feeling the same closeness they once shared, and desperately trying to keep Catherine away from her influence. Cassie had frightened her deeply then, just as she frightened how now. Her height of anger had been profane and as much as Phil hated to admit it, she sincerely wished they had not reunited the friendship.

All thoughts were broken as Cassie pranced in, an unnatural and sickening grin affixed on her face. "Who's for coffee?" They both declined, she shrugged and sat down looking from one to the other. Don finally spoke first, breaking the air of tension, "I didn't see Skye or Roger at the funeral. Are they coming here for the wake?"

Cassie shook her head slowly, "No Skye took the news very badly I'm afraid, she told Jake that under no circumstances could she bring herself to come. And Roger naturally stayed to console his wife."

"Yes, that's understandable. Is anyone else coming back?"

She let out a low throaty laugh; Phil felt nauseas at the sound. "No. Most of the people there were Rae's friends and I believe they were all going back to her parent's house for their wake. So I'm afraid it's just us, and as Jake most probably won't show his face, we may as well make the most of it."

This was more than Philyce could bear. She was actually talking as though they were having a party, instead of just returning from burying the mangled remains of a small innocent child. "Don I really think we should be going. I don't want to leave Catherine too long with the babysitter since I don't really know her that well."

Cassie looked at them with feigned hurt and disappointment, "No, please don't go. Since the children are with their Mother, and Jake is buried away in the bedroom, I don't want to be alone. Please, please don't go." Philyce looked at her astounded, one minute she's as happy as a lark, now she's mournful and pleading for them to stay.

"No, honestly Cassie, I can't leave Catherine too long."

Don took his wife's hand, "Why don't you go honey, I'll stay a little longer and Cassie can drive me home later," he looked towards her for assent, she nodded;

"Sure that would be no problem at all."

Philyce looked at each in turn, she felt a chill ease along her spine. How could he possibly wish to stay with this demented woman, no matter how earnest her pleas were? And hadn't they planned to take their daughter on a picnic to take their minds off this morning's events, "But Don, I thought …"

He nodded, "Yes dear, but we can do that anytime. I really think Cassie needs a friendly shoulder to lean on today."

"Well if you've made plans, please don't let me spoil them," Cassie stated with feigned sadness.

He reached across and took her hand in his, patting it gently, "Don't be silly, we were only going on a picnic, and we can do that another day."

They walked Phil to her car, and watched as she tore off down the road, a little too fast Cassie thought. It was obvious she wasn't at all impressed with these arrangements, but too bad, she had a baby daughter to go home to. And what did she have? Nothing.

Instead of moving back to the house, she took his hand and led him towards the crops. "I hope you don't mind but I really don't feel like sitting inside that tomb," she pointed to the house; "I just feel like walking amongst the vegetables where life is abundant, away from the doom and gloom of my husband."

"You don't seem terribly sympathetic Cassie. I mean you could hardly expect Jake to be galloping for joy, plus, I'm sure he must be harboring an awful lot of guilt."

She came to an abrupt halt, spun around and faced him with eyes of fire, "I lost a child also Don, but I didn't spit the dummy and start knocking my head against walls, or rolling around the bed wallowing in self pity. At least Jake had Carly for seven years, I didn't even get the chance to HOLD my child, let alone see him grow and develop his own personality. I'm afraid Jake is a poor excuse for a man. Always has been and always will be."

With as much speed as a raging fire when the wind changes, her expression altered and an impish grim curled her lips; she pointed towards the packing shed; "Jake has an old mattress in there. Let's go in and make love."

He couldn't believe his ears; what sort of woman could be that callous at a time like this. She showed no remorse and most certainly no concern for her husband. "Honestly dear, I hardly think this is the time or place for that. In fact I think we'd better get back to the house in case Jake needs you."

"Oh come on, don't be such a baby. It'll be fun. Besides Jake took some tablets as soon as we got home and by now he'll be sleeping with princess valium and most definitely out for the count and snoring like a Mac Truck," she stated without one iota of compassion.

Words eluded him, this was not right, *she* was not right, he knew this was as wrong as it could get, yet with the reluctance of a man being led to the gallows, he yielded and silently followed.

Jake woke in a bath of perspiration, the name Carly dwindling from his lips as he sat upright. The same recurring nightmare that had tormented him during the hours of darkness for the past week was now haunting him through the day. How could he go on with the vision of her broken and bloody body burned deep into his memory? They say time heals all wounds, but how could time possibly erase the guilt and horrific recollections of that day. Swinging his legs over the side of the bed, he attempted to stand, however the effects of the drug he had taken still hadn't worn off completely and the floor came crashing up to meet him. Oblivious to the pain, he lay there allowing the tears to cascade down his face without shame. Why hadn't he taken more interest in what Carly was saying to him that day, instead of being so damned preoccupied about Cassie leaving him? That would have been a far easier thing to accept than this.

After several minutes he managed to pull himself up, and staggered into the bathroom. Only after a very long time of standing under the shower allowing the cool water wash away the heaviness of the valium, the tears and the sweat, did it occur to him how silent the house was. Where was Cassie? Didn't Don and Philyce come back to the house after the funeral? Where were they? He felt confused, so damn confused. Maybe it was the next day and Cassie was at work, or maybe he had been asleep for a week. He didn't know; the days and nights seemed to merge these days. It could be the middle of the bloody year for all he knew or really cared.

Once he dressed, he walked into the kitchen and sat down. The clock on the wall told him it was three in the afternoon. Where was everyone? Don and Philyce had come back he knew that for a fact; surely they wouldn't have left already. Hitting his forehead with the palm of his hand, he once again struggled to remember what day it was. Those damn pills were the cause of this memory lapse. They were turning his brain into confetti. Yet without them he couldn't sleep, he couldn't even close his eyes without Carly's face screaming up at him, accusing him, "It's *YOUR fault Daddy; you killed me!*" she would say. And he had, just as surely as if had taken a gun to her head, he had killed her.

John Yates had been arrested and charged that same day, but that didn't matter, it was still his own stupid fault she was on the road, it was *he* who had given her the skates; it was *he* who was not supervising her not John Yates. He rose and moved to the window staring far to the left where the edges of his crops were visible. Who had been tending the soil, picking the tomatoes and the like? Who had delivered the vegetables to the markets? Who? Was it David? Or did he do it. Jake left the kitchen and moved outside, where all his pent up frustration and anger took its toll. Very slowly he raised his arms to the fiery face of the sun, turned to the North and screamed.

It was the scream of a mad man, or perhaps a wild animal caught in a trap. Don sat upright, startled. He glanced at Cassie asleep beside him; her smooth and naked skin glistened seductively with beads of perspiration. He felt physically sick. One of his best friends lay in the house grieving for his dead daughter, while he screws his wife under his very nose, on his own property. It wasn't right. And even though his morals had dropped by his lust for Jake's wife, this would have to be the lowest any man could go. It took a lot of effort for Don to raise his stout little body off the mattress on the floor, but after a few grunts and groans he finally managed it, then struggled into the trousers that he was certain had recently shrunk. Cassie stirred and rolled over, her arm automatically reaching out for him. Panic filled his throat, he wanted to get away before she woke; he couldn't explain the reason he had decided to walk home was because during the last two hours his desire for her had turned into vile disgust. With his shoes still in his hands, he moved to the door; and recoiled instantly as Jake's stooped form ambled slowly towards him.

Panic soared through his veins; "Crap in a bucket!!" He was a renown fast talker but an extremely slow mover, however, he managed to run to the window, lever himself up and out with the agility of a teenager, and had reached the road as Jake did the shed.

The sight of her lying as bare as the day she was born brought an ache to his groin. It had been a long time since he had touched her and for a moment almost forgot his grief. As though feeling his gaze she opened her eyes expecting to see Don; blind panic struck at the sight of Jakes' tortured face stared back at her. Her arm instinctively fell to the side Don had been laying; it was empty. Cassie sighed with relief however, now an explanation was going to be required.

"What are you doing in here, naked?" he asked casually; a little too casually; she felt sick.

Obviously Don had escaped, either that or he was well hidden either way she exhaled with relief, "I didn't want to disturb you while you were sleeping so peacefully," It was the first thing she could think of and knew even Jeffrey could have come up with a better one that that.

"That's absurd Cassie; there are two spare bedrooms in the house."

"Yes I'm perfectly aware of that Jake, I just felt I needed my own space and you needed yours" that sounded ridiculous and she knew it, however, he seemed to be accepting it. Although he did raise one eyebrow and glance suspiciously at her naked body, "I know what you're thinking; that I'm losing my mind lying here naked, but it was just so damned hot it was the only way I could sleep. He seemed to be buying it and when he turned and slowly walked away she sighed with relief.

By the time Don got home his feet were swollen with blisters. He eased off his shoes the moment he entered the foyer and hobbled into the kitchen, where Philyce sat staring daggers. "So, did you have a nice afternoon comforting Cassie," the sarcasm was obvious, he shrugged, "It was alright. We talked for a bit, and then Cassie fell asleep in the lounge chair, so I walked home."

She glanced at his red swollen feet and gasped, "Oh for goodness sake Don, why the hell didn't you call me to pick you up?"

He shrugged, then extracted a shallow basin from beneath the sink, filled it with cold water and sat opposite her submerging his aching feet into the cool welcoming liquid. "Honestly Don, I can't believe you fell for that little performance she put on for our benefit. Surely you must have noticed her composure at the cemetery. There was no way that woman was even slightly upset, and don't dare tell me she was!"

The bitterness was spewing forth like a boiling radiator, he looked at her surprised, "I thought Cassie was your best friend, but you're speaking as though she's your worst enemy."

Philyce threw herself back in the chair, and raising her eyes to the ceiling, sighed, "She was. But things are different now, she's changed." She stood and moved crouching beside him, "I told you what happened at the hospital when she knew she was losing her baby." He nodded, "Well ever since then she scares me. I can't explain it, but there's something different about her Don; something really quite evil and irrational. In fact I would go so far as to say I think Cassie is quite insane, and I really feel we should seriously consider keeping right away from her. And I think you should let fire her!"

Don's mind wandered back over the past month. He had noticed changes in Cassies moods; happy, then with the blink of eye sad, then five minutes later, distant as though she was on another planet. The cause of these drastic changes, he had assumed was because she and Jake were having problems. And, then there was this afternoon. Her obvious aggression towards Jake had disturbed him, yet he still allowed her to seduce him only minutes later. Philyce was right, Cassie was not well, and they should keep their distance. "I agree dear. I will ring her tomorrow and tell her you've decided you want your job back. You need have no more to do with her if you so wish, I won't pressure you. However, I intend to keep in touch with Jake. That poor bastard has been to hell and back, and I think he can probably use all the friends he can get right now; especially now!"

Dane sat in the corner of the large lounge room with Jeffrey, while his Grandparents tried unsuccessfully to entertain the bevy of mourners moving around in slow motion around the room. His Mother had taken Felicity into the bedroom hours before, and still hadn't returned. He assumed she was asleep.

"Of course you realize this is all *HER* fault," he whispered to Jeff. The small boy looked up at his older brother in a daze. This was all too much for him. He had never seen his mother cry so much. He had never cried so much, and now Dane was talking in riddles.

"What's whose fault?" Dane waved his arms around the room,

"All of this is Cassies' fault.

Jeffrey looked perplexed, "I know I'm only a kid Dane, but how can you blame her? She wasn't driving the car that hit Carly."

An irritable eyebrow lifted and he sighed with impatience, "Bad things have started happening to our family since *SHE* came on the scene. Dad doesn't care about us anymore; he always takes her side and blames us when things go wrong. And, now this has happened. Remember the Ouija board?"

His brother nodded, "It tried to warn Carly of danger. Maybe we are all in danger while she's in our house." Jeffrey screwed up his face in an ungainly manner;

"I think you've been watching too many horror movies Dane. Dad doesn't blame *US* when things go wrong; he blames *YOU*; mostly because it *IS* your fault. You don't like Cassie so you always give her a hard time. Then because Dad gets mad, you reckon it's her fault." The sudden need to defend his Stepmother became overwhelming, and the isolated expression of despair across Dane's face brought triumph to his heart. "That stupid whatever you call it board was a trick. And I still reckon you were pushing it. How do we know you're not the one bringing bad things to our family?"

Even though he knew he was pushing Dane to the limit he kept going, "You've been trying to get us to do horrible things to her ever since she moved in. Like that time you wanted me to catch that big hairy spider and put it in her bed. And because I said no, you broke my Action Man. You're a sicko Dane, a real sicko."

That was the last straw; Dane drew his hand back and let Jeffrey have it right across his face. Jeffrey bolted, sobbing, into the arms of his Grandmother. Then he simply stood, hands in pocket and slipped out the back door before Moya could reproach him. He *HATED* Jeffrey. He *HATED* them all, and as soon as he could save up enough money, he was going.

Don rang early the next morning. Cassie could barely drag herself from the bed to answer the phone. With Jake's constant tossing and turning and screaming in his sleep, she had managed to shut her eyes for only a couple of hours.

His voice was stiff and formal, "I'm sorry Cassie, but Philyce has decided she wants her job back, and since there's not enough work for both of you, I'm afraid I won't be needing you anymore."

Her initial shock was obvious. There was something wrong. Why hadn't he mentioned that yesterday? After a moment she responded calmly, "I see; what about us Don?" Even though his silence more or less answered her, she waited patiently, feeling the rage of a cyclone building deep in the pit of her stomach. He cleared his throat, "I think perhaps you should try and work things out with your husband."

"As I recall it, you made the first move," she whispered between clenched teeth.

"Yes, well, you fascinated me, you were a challenge. I wanted to know if you were as efficient in bed as you were with everything else. And now that my curiosity is appeased there is no sense in carrying on a meaningless relationship."

She felt her body sway, her fury was so enveloping it hurt. "Well, this is one *HELL* of a time for true confessions, you smutty little bastard!" The receiver fell into the cradle with an almighty crash, and then with one swift blow the entire instrument was sent flying against the wall. *"Bastard, Bastard!"* she screamed.

Jake was aroused from his nightmare by the sound of something heavily hitting the wall followed by profound swearing. He jumped from the bed and ran into the lounge room. Cassie was pacing the floor holding her head with her hands. Her long nightdress swirled and twirled savagely as she moved faster and faster.

"What the hell is going on?"

Throwing her arms in the air then making a fist and punching her thigh she yelled *"He fired me! The prick fired me!"*

"Who did? Don?"

"Yes Don; who else do I work for?!"

"Well that's hardly the end of the world Cassie. You've still got my business to run, and if that's not enough, you can always find something else."

"Yes, you're right. Of course, you're right." The tempest over, she drew a deep breath and moved to the kitchen; "Want some coffee?"

Jake stared after her amazed. He had never seen such violence diminish so rapidly. Perhaps the strain of Carly's death and the pressure of the funeral had taken its toll. He had been so engrossed in his own misery he hadn't even stopped to consider how Cassie was coping. They hadn't been out for months; perhaps tonight would be the perfect time to rectify that. "Cass, we've all been under a lot of duress. Why don't we go out to dinner tonight and try and put our lives back into some sort of perspective?"

"Darn, I forgot, we're all out of coffee; how about tea?" He nodded and sat at the table, "You haven't answered me Cass." Positioning herself opposite him, she gave him an insipid grin; "It's a nice thought honey, but Rae's bringing the kids home today; remember."

"Yes I know. The children have been under just as much pressure as we have. I think a night out would do them good also."

"Oh I see, I thought you meant just us. Sure Jake, we can all go to the Pizza Place or somewhere like that. Or maybe Chinese would be nice." Jake watched her face contort into different expressions; she seemed far, far away from where he was.

"Actually Cassie, I was thinking more along the lines of a nice Italian restaurant or something in that category."

"Well, whatever, it's all the same to me. I have a million things to do so I'd better get started."

He folded his arms and watched intently as she bustled about the kitchen cleaning things that didn't need it. He was beginning to worry about her. He was very worried.

Carl drove Rae back with the children at around four fifteen that afternoon. She faced Jake with such a defiant twist to her mouth; he thought she was going to spit at him. "I've told the kids to collect their things. As of now, they live with me."

He stared at her motionless for about thirty seconds. *"Like Hell!"*

"There's no point in arguing Jake. It is my opinion our offspring are no longer safe in this environment."

Carl ushered the children into their rooms, away from the arguing adults. He had listened to his daughter rant and rave all day, and he knew she would never pull this one off. Even if Jake conceded to her fetish, he knew within a week she would be bringing them back.

"You can't take my children away from me now Rae. *NOT NOW!* Please Carl tell her she can't do this."

The outraged woman ignored his plea; I can and I am. It is obvious the lack of supervision in this house is perilous for my children. At least with me their safety will be ensured."

Cassie stood in the background, while Rae focusing

her eyes directly at her. Jake grabbed her shoulders roughly, turning her to face him, "After all these years of not caring, of hardly even seeing them, how can you actually have the audacity to suggest you would be a better parent." She flinched in pain as his forefinger began deliberate abuse against her shoulder blade, "You relinquished custody when you turned your back and walked out on all of us. If you want them now, you will have to take me to Court and fight for them. Because there is absolutely no way I will let them walk out of here with you!" He pushed her away with contempt and turned to Carl, "You're a bloody cop, what rights do I have?" The elderly man with legs astride and arms behind his back, looked from one to the other, "I'm sorry Rae, but Jake does have a valid case. You were the one that left them in his care, and, you *HAVE* had ample time to take custody, but have chosen not to. And, I can assure you no Judge in this state would agree with your ridiculous notion, that because Carly met with a fatal accident, the rest of the children are in danger. She wasn't murdered Rae, it could have happened under your watch also."

Rae gave her Father an insidious look, "Are my ears deceiving me, or are you actually siding with *HIM!?*"

Carl brought his hands to his hips, "I'm not siding with anyone. I'm stating facts Rae. I tried to tell you all this earlier on, but as always, you're too pig headed to listen. Plain and simply Jake is correct in his reasoning. In the Judge's eyes you *HAVE* neglected the children, and every time I've suggested you take the children to live with you, you've *ALWAYS* said you're too busy. You've even been too bloody busy to see them on a regular basis. In all the years you've been gone, how many times would you say you've seen them?' She stared at him blankly, "I'll bet you a thousand dollars, you could count them on one hand. So how do you think that would look in Court?"

"*THEY'RE MY* children and I have the right," she stated bitterly.

Patience was not one of Carl's better assets, he sighed heavily, "Your unit is sparsely furnished, there is not enough bedrooms. Are you telling me, you finally have enough money to move into a bigger home, and are now financially able to support them?"

"Well, no, not yet. But they could live with you and Mum until I am."

"And there it is Rae; once again you're passing them on to someone else. The Judge isn't going to take the children away from a loving caring Father to live with Grandparents especially because there is no cause. Carly died and everyone here is devastated but it was an accident Rae. However if you still want to fight for custody, then you'd better get yourself financially organized. Otherwise forget it."

If looks could kill, everyone in that room would have been dead. She glared at each of them with profound loathing, grabbed her bag and flounced out of the door. Carl looked at Jake, smiled and patted him on the shoulder with a warning: "Just because I was on your side this time doesn't mean I would be when and If Rae finally gets herself a real job, a larger home and money in the bank." One final pat on the back and nod to Cassie and he was gone.

Cassie threw her arms in the air and squealed with delight, "Way to go Carl!" Boy did he give it to her right between the eyes!"

Jake, however, was hesitant, "Yes he did, this time. But you heard him Cassie; if she gets financially set and wants to fight us it's going to be a whole different game of cards. However no matter what it takes or how much, I vow; I will fight her. There's no way that woman is going to take my children off me, not now."

Chapter 16

Ocher and russet leaves fell lazily to the earth, blanketing the roads and lawns. The sun baked days of summer had long lapsed and the cool crisp breeze of autumn now took its place. It had been fifteen months since that awful day of the funeral and Rae's threats, which, as predicted never eventuated. But, at least now she took the children for weekends on a regular basis. Jake was slowly coming to terms with his grief and seemed to cope alright during the day, but it was at night when the nightmares started where he could see his daughter crumpled and torn over and over that kept him in torment.

Cassie moved to the kitchen window; Felicity and Jeffrey played happily on a second hand swing Jake had bought for them recently. Dane sat further afield in a world of his own. She wondered what sort of things crossed the boys mind when he sat as a recluse day after day. Even today, his eighteenth birthday, made no difference. Jake said it was because of Carly's death, but she knew better; she was the thorn in his side and he would not alter his mind or mood until she was gone. She smiled "And Hell would freeze over before that happened!"

Jake came from behind and placed his arms around her waist. "It's a shame Don and Philyce can't make it tonight." Their very name brought a tyrannous twist to her mouth. If only he knew, but he didn't. He had no idea she had confronted Philyce in her home a week after Don had fired her. "What the hell is going on?" she had demanded, while her stunned friend had looked on open mouthed, "I haven't the faintest idea what you're talking about," she had finally spat out.

"Oh come off it Phil. Give me a little bit of credit will you. You've been avoiding me for months. You haven't bothered to return any of my calls. I saw the look you gave Don the day of the funeral when I asked you to come back. That excuse you gave was pitiful; and speaking of Don all of a sudden *YOU* want your job back so he fires me, then Skye happens to go into his office and discovers an 18 year old girl working for him: So I'll ask you again, *"WHAT is going on!!"*

Philyce instinctively looked around for some form of weapon. This woman terrified her and with her mind as irrational as it was, there was no telling what she was capable of. Picking up a wooden Madonna that took pride of place on the side board, she confronted her face on. "Alright Cassie, you want to know why I've been avoiding you, I'll tell you. I don't trust you anymore, you've changed somehow. There's something evil in the way you think, the way you speak sometimes, and quite frankly I don't care to keep your company anymore. You frighten me Cass, you really frighten me!"

Cassie released a low harsh laugh, "You're not serious. We're friends Phil, remember. And you don't need your stupid little statue; I'm not going to hurt you.

"Perhaps not physically, but mentally you never seem to stop hurting me." She noticed Cassies' eyebrows rise; "Yes that's right Cass, I know about you and my husband. He told me everything. At first I didn't believe him, but then I thought well, if she can do it once she can do it again. No Cass, you *WERE* my friend, but not anymore. You'll see us occasionally, but *ONLY* because Don wants to keep in touch with Jake." Philyce saw the instant look of concern cross Cassies face and smiled; for once she had something over her; "Don't worry he's not going to say anything to Jake; he doesn't give a rats about you but he doesn't want to break Jakes heart!" With that said, she picked up Cassies bag and handed it to her, "Now, I would like you to leave, and please do not return unless you are invited."

She didn't care about them, and so long as Don remained quiet about their affair, everything would be alright. Besides there were more important matters to deal with, this blasted party for one.

Jake kissed her neck, she jumped startled. Having been so absorbed in her thoughts, she had forgotten he was there. "There are still a few hours before things get under way, and since the kids are occupied outside, what about coming into the bedroom with me?" He lifted his eyebrows twice and wiped his tongue around his lips in a very suggestive manner. Without answering she took his hand and led him into the bedroom. Everything was automatic. They both removed their clothes and lay on the bed. Jake was like a teenager doing it for the first time; he was doing his best to arouse her, but he was clumsy and awkward, and when he pummeled her breasts it was like a baker kneading dough, she cried out in pain. "Sorry" he whispered and moved his hands between her thighs. His penetration was very rough and she had to stop herself from screaming "Get off you are hurting me!" however within a minute it was over and he rolled off. Cassie felt as though she had just been raped and was trying very hard not to cry.

The party could hardly have been considered a raging success. The few friends Dane had invited sat in the lounge quietly as though they were in Church. Cassie looked around; this was ridiculous; not only did she feel as though she was back in the morgue, the birthday boy hadn't even bothered to make an appearance. Moving to the kitchen window she peered out into the semi darkness. His tall shadow stood beside the swing, one hand clung to the chain, while his head was bent, obviously in deep thought. Skye came up beside her; "He's a worry isn't he?" Cassie smiled but did not respond; he was a worry but not in the sense Skye meant. The middle aged woman sighed, "There is so much anger in that boy, so much hatred. It simply isn't healthy for a lad of his age. Why do you suppose he holds so much resentment?"

She shrugged, "Because of me." She faced her friend, "Even after all these years, he has never accepted me, or forgiven his Father for marrying me. I don't suppose I can blame him, all children no matter how old want their Father and Mother to be together." She sighed; "But my friend, that is his problem, not ours, so come on let's get a drink and see if we can give this party a bit of life."

When Dane came into the kitchen for breakfast the next morning, his Father sat at the table tapping his cup with a pen. The veins in his neck seemed to throb in time with his heart beat; Dane knew he was in trouble *again*. He poured himself a juice and sat opposite waiting for the eruption; it didn't happen, instead Jake glanced at him briefly, then back to the cup, there was no roar, "It was a nice party last night. Pity you missed it." Dane swung his leg across the corner of the table; an action he knew would send his Father into a rage. However, the gesture was ignored; instead Jake moved his own leg across the other corner. His voice was soft yet menacing, "You know, if it hadn't been for Cassie and Skye acting the goat and getting your friends up to dance, I'm quite certain the party would have been over by nine o'clock.

The boy shrugged, "Yeah, so what!" Jake stared at him in disbelief, "So what! It was your eighteenth! You were supposed to be living it up, not standing outside in the dark, while your friends sat inside in a coma. Most boys get drunk on their eighteenth. Believe it or not, they actually have fun!"

A fire simmered in his veins, and as his blood reached boiling point, he jerked his legs from the table, stood and slammed his fist into the refrigerator behind, "Well Dad, I'm not *MOST* boys, I'm *ME*. I didn't ask for a damn party, and since I didn't want it in the first place, entertaining those ass holes was your concern, *NOT MINE!*" His Father's eyes grew black, his jaw jerked spasmodically, then pushing back roughly from the table; moved to his son grabbing and bunching his T shirt in his fist then pulled the boy inches from his face, "*Now you wait just a minute young man!*" The youth shoved him harshly away, "No, *YOU* wait a bloody minute. You haven't bothered with anything concerning me since," he turned his head towards the back, where Cassie hung out the washing; "Since Madam Muck out there came on the scene. Did you really think giving me a stupid party, was going to make up for the last few years. If you really want to make me happy, get rid of *HER!*" Stars circled in front of his eyes from the blow his Father released; Dane rubbed his jaw, "That's right Dad, punch me again, stick up for her; *you always do*!" Jake stood back stunned as Dane left through the front door, slamming it dramatically behind.

"Push me higher" Felicity screamed happily to her brother. Cassie glanced towards the swing, where Jeffrey, looking bored to death stood patiently pushing his sister. "When is it going to be my turn?" he complained.

Higher and higher she soared. The sky was the limit, she let one hand go reaching out for it, "Look Jeff I can almost touch the clouds!" she screeched.

Cassie became alarmed and shouted; "Don't push her any higher Jeffrey; Felicity hold on with *BOTH* hands!!! She screamed. It was too late; the little girl was like a bird flying high towards the Heavens. There was nothing around her, no confines, only the grayness from above beckoning. The earth below turned as she somersaulted, the trees flashing past were a blur. Jeffrey was screaming hysterically, Cassie was running her arms held out to catch the falling child; she reached her as the child hit the ground. Nothing, there was nothing but darkness, silent, painless darkness.

Jake heard his son scream, he heard Cassie shouting then scream out; his blood froze, goose bumps covered his skin. His limbs wouldn't work. He felt as though he was moving in slow motion; it seemed to take forever to reach the back door. The swing still moved slightly, one chain dragging on the lawn, while the wooden seat stared back at him, limp and lifeless. Everything seemed animated, he felt as though he was in a book. Cassie was screaming for him to call an ambulance. It couldn't be happening, not again."

She was buried beside her sister. Jake stared at the two small plots, he couldn't cry. There were no tears left to shed, a numbed incomprehension had taken its place. He felt like a man drowning, every time he came up for air, something happened to push him down again. He couldn't believe it; first Carly, her small body completely shattered, now his baby, her neck broken, her spinal cord completely snapped. What was going on? What had he done throughout his life that was so bad, to be punished in this way?

Rae on her knees, moaned beside him. He glanced down to her fragile form rocking and swaying with pain. A black veiled hat concealed her eyes, but he knew she was, as he was, numb and tearless.

Cassie stood behind Jeffrey with her hands on his small quivering shoulders. The tears were rolling down her cheeks freely. This little child had been prepared to put aside her beloved doll for her baby. She was the only one Cassie really cared about. It wasn't fair, it should have been Dane. That rotten mongrel had no compassion at all. He had come home the afternoon of the accident, been told, then promptly left and hadn't been seen since. He offered no words of comfort to his Father or Mother, and hadn't even bothered to turn up the funeral.

When they left the cemetery, it was separately; Cassie with Jeffrey, Jake with Rae. She watched as they walked to the hearse. Rae clung desperately to her ex husband and Cassie experienced a very brief but definite stirring of jealousy. At Rae's request there was to be no wake this time; only family attended the small service. She couldn't cope with the trauma of mounds of faces kissing her lightly on the cheek; sympathizing and pitying her and whispering behind their hands as she walked by. No, this time she would suffer alone. Even when Jake offered to see her home, she had refused. It was only through his continual insistence she had relented.

He followed her slowly into the small unit, which, after all this time, was still cold and lacking in most furniture. The focal point of the room was an easel, with a covered painting on it. He lifted the sheet and stared for a very long time at the canvas. It seemed almost three dimensional; simple but beautiful; a beach, and the faces of three of his children were drawn into the bodies of seagulls, flying above the spray of the surf which almost seemed to spray from the canvas; all except Carly. Her beautiful eyes staring back at him from the centre of the scene, reaching out to him, ringlets of gold framing her oval face and large tear drops sprinkled her cheeks like diamonds. "I did that twelve months ago, and haven't done anything since," Rae explained from behind. Jake swung around and grabbed her, pulling her into his arms. He felt her body soften and begin to shake with the onset of suppressed grief.

She held him tightly, feeling the loneliness of all these months melt away in his embrace. "What's happening Jake, what's happening to our children?" she sobbed into his shoulder.

He stroked her hair softly; "I don't know honey, I honestly don't know." They clung to each other, absorbing each others' strength for what seemed to Jake like hours. He traced his finger over the line of her chin, "Would you like me to stay with you tonight?" he whispered softly. She assented with a smile, then her face creased with lines of scorn, "What about your wife?"

For some reason, at that precise moment, Jake felt as though Cassie was somewhere in the back of a dream. He wasn't married to her, and Rae was his wife. "She'll understand," he whispered pulling Rae back into his arms.

They sat up talking into the early hours of the morning. "Do you realize Jake, this is the first time since before we were married, we have actually conversed without arguing." She moved to his side and touched his face gently, "Do you suppose this means, that now, we would be mature enough to have and hold a relationship together.

The tired lines around his eyes widened as he looked at her amazed, "I'm not sure I understand; what exactly are you saying Rae?"

"Leave her Jake. Bring Jeffrey and Dane away from there. The four of us can make a new life somewhere. I know we can, things are different now; we seem bonded somehow."

Jake smiled, took her hand to his lips and kissed it softly, "Rae, the only bond we are sharing at the moment is our grief. In a few years time when the pain has eased, everything would be just the same as it was before. You and I have different wants and needs. It wouldn't work honey, it couldn't. We were kids when we fell in love, and everything seemed achievable; and we ventured into marriage with rose colored glasses, but we have different concepts Rae, that's why it didn't work the first time. And that's why it wouldn't work now. Come now, I think we should try and get some sleep."

They snuggled together on Rae's double bed fully clothed, and, for the first time in a very long time, he didn't have nightmares.

Jake took a taxi and arrived home around nine thirty that morning. Cassie lay on the settee still wearing the black dress she had worn to the funeral. She raised herself up on one elbow as he entered; "Did you get lost?"

"No, we needed that time together Cass. I don't know if you can understand, but she was *OUR* baby, and the only comfort we could draw, was from each other."

"Did you sleep with her?" Jake gave her a disgusted look, "Yes but not in the way you're thinking; we lay together and slept in each other's arms and that's as far as it went!"

She felt ashamed, or was it guilt from her own transgressions; "Would you like some coffee?"

He nodded then pointed to her attire, "You obviously haven't been to bed yet. Why?"

"Jeffrey had a terrible night. Cried for hours, and then started screaming he was going to be next. It was awful Jake. In the end I gave him half a valium, and decided to wait up for you. I really wish you had called me Jake."

"I know; I'm sorry. Any sign of Dane?" He was changing the subject and she knew it, "No nothing."

Dane made his appearance the next day. He was unshaven and extremely dirty. When he walked past, Jake held his nose. "Where the hell have you been, you smell like a hamster cage?"

The boy cast him an abrasive glance, "I've been around. And since I'm eighteen, *it's none of your business!*" Jake was far too exhausted to argue, he accepted this without question, and left him alone.

Chapter 17

Carl stopped by Rae's unit a week later. She had requested time to herself, but he considered seven days long enough to mourn in solitude. With one hand on his hip and the other rubbing his chin, he stared at the canvas in the same manner Jake had. Only now, Felicity's face had been removed from the seagull's body, and been enlarged and brought in next to Carly's.

"A little morbid isn't it?" She shook her head, "No; I don't think so. I'm going to name it 'Free Souls'. You see, Jeffrey and Dane are still in the birds' bodies, but Carly and Felicity are free of confinement." He glanced at his daughter with a remissive frown, "I still think it's morbid."

"Well I suppose you would. After all you'd really need to have an artists' imagination to appreciate the context of the painting." There was a moment of silence before she took her Father's hand and led him to a chair, and crouching beside him placed one hand on his knee, "I want to get a regular job Dad. I want to earn as much money as I can, as quickly as I can."

He looked at her suspiciously; "Why the sudden change of mind?"

"I want my two sons Dad," she paused, he was not going to like what followed, "And, I want Jake back; I have realized *I still love him!*"

Instead of the outburst of rage she expected, he remained calm, sighing softly; "Yes precious I thought this might happen. It's amazing what grief can do to people." Her eyes widened in surprise, "Why do you say that?"

"When parents experience the devastation of losing a child, they automatically feel drawn together. In your case, you've lost two children within two years, and, just because you're divorced don't mean you wouldn't feel that same heartbreak. It's that invisible cord of helplessness and despair that joins you together spiritually; sweetheart that's what you are mistaking for love; but, baby girl trust me; it will pass and gradually you will realize your feelings are simply based on the loss the two of you share," he kissed her cheek softly and wiped a tear away with his hand.

She rose and moved to the canvas, staring at it; "That's basically what Jake said, but I disagree. There's more to it," she faced him again, "I can feel it Dad, and he's changed. He seems more mature, more responsible somehow, and I honestly believe I've fallen in love with him again."

Carl smiled, "Has it occurred to you his wife might be responsible for his change?"

"*No!* I won't believe that for a moment. She's a witch, and, I mean that literally."

"Rae, honey," he got to his feet, crossing the room toward her, but when he tried to embrace her, she shrugged him away; "I'm getting him back Dad, it may take a while for him to see the truth, but I will get him back."

Carl shrugged and turned to the door, "Well all I can say is; good luck," and left.

The weeks rolled into months, Jake had fired his helping hands, insisting on doing all the work himself, and since he was gone before dawn and never home until the stars were set high in the sky, she was usually asleep when he fell into bed.

Much to her dismay, Rae had started seeing the two boys

every Saturday but the worst was to come, she insisted on staying there, rather than taking them to her unit; and; Cassie noticed Jake seemed to hang around the house on Rae's visits. Yet it wasn't until Rae invited herself to spend Christmas with them, she questioned her motives. Jake had taken the pick-up to the cannery when she arrived the Saturday before Christmas. Her eyes searched the rooms; Cassie spoke softly; slowly; "He's *NOT* here."

"Who do you mean?" Cassie wasn't buying it; the innocence in the voice made her want to vomit; she snapped; *"JAKE OF COURSE!"*

Rae looked affronted, "I'm here to see my sons, not my ex-husband."

Cassie scowled; *"Really!!* Well you're out of luck there also. Dane is, goodness knows where, and Jeffrey spent the night at a friend's house and since *Jake* spoke to the boys' Mother I'm not sure if he's home tonight or not; so I guess there's really no point for you to hang around here, is there!?"

Rae seemed to be oblivious to Cassies' sharp rhetoric and placed her bag on the table, "Oh I think there is; after all it *IS* Saturday, and they both know I'll be here today, so, I'll just wait; if you don't mind that is, but, please go on with whatever you were doing, there's no need to entertain me."

Eyes flashing precariously, Cassie glared until Rae's cheeks reddened and she looked away uncomfortably; only then did she return to the kitchen. At least she had let Rae know silently that she did mind, so Jake could not accuse her of being rude.

Jeffrey meandered in an hour later, and ran into his Mother's arms. Cassie felt her stomach turn with loathing. How dare this woman walk into *HER* house and make her feel like the intruder. Her mood was only appeased when they left hand in hand to walk amongst the gardens.

Cassie had taken a plate of sandwiches out to them at

about 1pm when Jake returned but there was still no sign of Dane. He kissed her briefly on the forehead, "I see Rae's car is here, where is she?"

"Outside with Jeffrey" then moved to the kitchen window as Jake instantly headed for the back door. Rae's face lit up when she saw him, and the hunger in her eyes could not be hidden. It was outrageous and must be stopped. She was too close for things to get stuffed up now. Jake said something to Jeff, and ruffled his hair, the next second the boy had left them alone. Jake took his seat and clasped Rae's hand. Cassie's heart was hitting her ribs, her stomach a large knot. Fifteen minutes later Jake came in to shower; Rae followed, and as she walked past Cassie at the sink gave her a victorious grin. Cassie instantly grabbed her arm spinning her around to face her front on. "Tell me again you are not interested *MY* husband."

The delicate woman flashed her perfect teeth, "Well I feel honoured; you are actually feeling threatened by me."

"Don't be ridiculous; what an absurd thing to say. Let me warn you, you are wasting your time. Jake *LOVES ME*; and any illusions you may have are just that!" Her voice was trembling and her hands cold and clammy.

Rae snickered breaking free; "Well then, you have nothing to worry about, do you?"

Cassie spent the rest of the afternoon lying in her room, her eyes unseeingly reading a book. She could hear their low voices talking and laughing in the kitchen, the sound of which made her nauseas. It was only when she heard the front door shut and her car start up, she came out. Jake was washing the coffee cups and singing softly to himself. "Well, you certainly seem in an extremely jovial mood."

He grinned, "That's because I am."

"Care to share; I could certainly use a laugh."

"It's nothing really," his grin broadened, "I'm just so

pleased to see Rae spending so much time with Jeff. He's such an impressionable kid; he really needs his Mother's influence right now."

She felt the soft sting of jealousy; isn't that what she'd been doing all this time; hadn't she been his Mother when 'the other one' was too busy with her painting. Deciding not to be childish she didn't relay those thoughts; instead unintentionally expressed her other side of jealousy; "Is that the only reason you're pleased to see your ex wife?" Her voice was edged with sarcasm.

Putting the cups down, he turned to her; "What exactly are you implying Cass?"

Avoiding the piercing gaze, she lowered her eyes, "Nothing; forget I said anything."

He placed a gentle hand under her chin tilting her face towards his, "What's the matter Cass? Is something bothering you?"

It took a moment, but she finally released her built up aggression; "Does *SHE* have to spend Christmas with us" Her presence makes me uncomfortable, and," she hesitated, "And, I don't think she comes here so much to see Jeff or Dane, it's more to see you."

He burst into laughter and pulled her into his arms, "You're jealous! You are actually jealous!"

Flying into a rage, she punched him in the chest, he pulled back gasping, yet continued to laugh. "I saw the way she looks at you. And, I saw you holding her hand earlier on. Not to mention the fact, you always seem to stay home when she's here. Go on, I defy you to deny your interest in her, or hers in you."

He was doubled over by now, his stomach hurt from laughing. Wiping the tears of joy, he motioned her to the kitchen table; when they were seated and he was composed enough to speak, he grabbed her hand, and, bringing it to his lips, kissed each finger, "I can't speak for Rae's feelings, but I can assure you I have absolutely no interest in her whatsoever. What you saw earlier, was me telling her exactly what I just told you, about how pleased I was she was spending time with Jeff. And as for me being around when she's here, it's purely coincidental. Nothing more, I promise. I love *YOU* Cass; don't you know that by now?" She smiled, but it was more for her ego than anything else. "Ok; but what about next week? Does she still have to spend Christmas with us?"

"Oh baby, where's the harm? Besides Jeffrey is really excited about it; you wouldn't want to disappoint him would you?"

However, Christmas was disappointing as was New Year, with everyone thinking of the year before, when Felicity was with them, and then, the year before that, with Carly. It seemed more of a wake than a celebration. Philyce rang one day early in the New Year catching Cassie off guard. Her voice was pleasant but formal; "Don would like you and Jake to attend a party we're having next Saturday. Can you make it, the boys are welcome, but I must warn you, there will be no other children their age here."

"I'll have to check with Jake, but I'm sure he has nothing planned. Dane can sit with Jeffrey and I'll bring a plate of sandwiches if you like."

"That's fine, see you around seven." The last thing Cassie felt like was seeing Philyce and Don. Yet for Jake's sake, she would have to make the supreme effort. He was still unaware of their confrontation, and she had no intention of telling him. Besides, he was already asking questions about their lack of communication, and by refusing this invitation, would only add further to his suspicion. She replaced the receiver gently, yes, they would have to attend this party, and further more she would have to pretend to be excited about it.

Chapter 18

Singing cicadas and chirping crickets filled the still, balmy night air with a rustic kind of music. It was already eight pm as Cassie decided to be fashionably late. Welcoming lights from their house spanned the road as they turned the corner; Cassie flinched; welcome for all except her that is. Jake's car had a flat battery, so they had taken hers. He felt ridiculous parking amidst the opulence and glamour of Porches, Mercedes and jazzy looking BMW sports models, so he parked their little Cortina further down the road.

The double doors were open and soft classical music drifted out to them. They entered without knocking and proceeded into the dining area. A large buffet adorned the Smokey glass table; Jake inhaled at the sight of crayfish, king prawns, smoked salmon and pate. Five types of exotic salads lay on a smaller table. Cassie giggled, all she had to offer was curried egg sandwiches; at which time she suddenly realized she had in fact forgotten to bring the damn things.

At that moment Don entered through French doors from the rear, "Hello there; glad you could make it" he took Jakes hand with a firm shake. Everybody is outside on the patio, please follow me. Phil's in the kitchen if you wish to say hello first Cass." She smiled politely; she certainly did not, but if she was to keep up with this ludicrous charade, she would have to. "Sure, I'll join you in a moment."

Jake accompanied Don outside; however, instead of retreating to the kitchen, Cassie decided to make the trip home to retrieve her forgotten sandwiches. One way to get even with these toffee noses, was to produce her 'egg sandwiches' and place them next to the caviar, oysters and the like; and chuckled with the thought of the silent gasps it would bring.

Within ten minutes she had returned, plate in hand. Philyce was still in the kitchen standing at the bench with her back to her. Cassie curled her lips into a forced smile and tapped her on the shoulder, "Hi".

The startled woman almost dropped the plate of canapés she had just picked up. "Hell Cassie you scared the living daylights out of me!"

She shrugged; "Sorry. Wow you look great!" she lied commenting on the fine red silk oriental dress she wore with a side split to the thigh.

"Thank you, so do you." Cassie automatically ran her hands down the slim line of her white pleated skirt, and blue roll neck blouse. She felt drab, looked drab and she knew Philyce knew it. But hey what the hell, she didn't have the money to squander on useless fashions, and wasn't about to waste what little they had on something she'd probably only wear once.

"I, put the sandwiches on the table. Quite a spread I must say," she was pointing to the dining room, Phil noticed blood on her right hand.

"Did you cut yourself or something?" Cassie looked at her hand and laughed, "No, actually I was going to steal a prawn, but it pricked me with its spike. So I guess that's what I get for trying to be sneaky eh?" Philyce wasn't the slightest bit amused, and forced a smile; "Would you like a bandage or something?"

"Hell no, it looks worse than it is. I'll just wash it and you'll never know it was there."

"Suit yourself. You know where the bathroom is; if you change your mind the bandages are in the last cupboard. I'll be outside when you're ready."

Cassie tried to mingle with the guests, but it was as she expected, they were all dressed up like Christmas tinsel and snobs to top it off. Finally, she found herself a chair in the corner and watched Jake conversing with a group of men in tuxedos near the pool. He stuck out like a sore thumb, dressed in plaid trousers and open neck shirt, and oh how she would love to walk up to them casually and push their upper class butts in the pool; the thought of which brought a rather devilish smile to her lips. A familiar voice brought her back from fantasy land; "What's so amusing?"

She jumped, and looked up at the tall thin form beside her. A light shone brightly above him, she had to squint to see who it was, "Roger? Oh thank heavens, a friendly face to rescue me from this miserable party. I didn't realize you were invited. Where's Skye?"

In a bid to slow down the interrogation, he raised his hands and laughed, "Wow. Firstly, I'm glad to see you to, secondly I wasn't exactly invited; I came to see Don about some business, so in effect I have gate crashed, and thirdly, Skye isn't here. So tell me, how are you and Jake coping these days?"

"We're managing. Each day gets a little easier. But I imagine it will be quite a few years before things even start to get back to normal."

At that moment Philyce interrupted their conversation, with the announcement of supper being served. They caught up with Jake at the table. "Roger, old man, how are you?" he asked shaking his hand and standing aside to allow access to the food. "Go for it man, there's a massive spread just waiting to be eaten."

Roger declined, "Oh no thanks; I'm not here to join the party. Actually, I'm trying to pin Don down for five minutes, and then I have to get back to my lovely wife." The elusive man approached at that moment; "Ah Don, can you spare me five?"

"Sure follow me into the study."

Cassie grabbed a plate and piled on the sea food. She noticed everyone bypassing her sandwiches, and chuckled, "Seems I should have brought caviar." Jake smiled; she was in an extremely good mood tonight.

"Never mind honey, you can't buy champagne on a beer budget. But one day we'll be part of the elite."

"What, and be part of this snobby crowd" Thanks, but no thanks. As a matter of fact, do you think it would be terribly rude of us to eat and run?"

He grimaced, "it sure would, but then who gives a rats. There are a couple of chairs over there. We can bolt down our food and then split."

The house was in darkness when they arrived home. Jake glanced at his watch. "Gosh it's only ten o'clock; very unusual for Dane to be asleep at this hour." They tip toed down the hall into their room. "I don't think they are asleep" she remarked placing an ear to the wall that joined the boys' room, "I can hear soft voices and music."

"It's probably the portable television. Dane has a very bad habit of leaving the damn thing on all night. I'll just go in and turn it off." He gave her an impish grin and lifted his eyebrows up and down, "Meanwhile, why don't you slip into something more comfortable, like, say; nothing!"

She had just sat on the bed and removed her shoes, when she heard his deathly scream. It penetrated her soul like electricity, sending static bolts through her body. A few seconds elapsed before her brain sent the message to her feet to move, and by the time she reached Jake he was vomiting on the floor. Waves of nausea rolled in her own stomach at the sight surrounding her. There was blood everywhere. Jeffrey's bed had been stripped of linen, and his mutilated body lay on the bloodied mattress.

"Where's Dane?" she screamed holding back the urge to vomit. Jake had fallen to the floor next to his son. He couldn't speak, he couldn't hear, he couldn't feel.

Instinctively Cassie ran into the girls' room, where he lay on the bed, eyes staring blindly at the ceiling. His breathing was so shallow she thought he was dead and screamed out for Jake; it took a second and he was there.

Jake thought he was dead also; "Dane!" he screamed. There was no response. She grabbed his wrist and felt for his pulse and sighed slightly relieved; "there's a pulse, very week but it is there. Call an ambulance Jake; *Hurry!*"

At that moment Dane groaned softly; she bent over him lifting his head slightly; it was a bloodless mask; "Why didn't they come for me? I waited but they didn't come."

"Who Dane; Who didn't come? She asked softly then looked towards Jake; who had covered his face with his hands and was crying openly.

"What the fuck is going on in this house??? I don't understand why me, why is this house taking all my children?"

He wasn't making sense and had covered his face with his hands, crying openly. *"Jake!"* she cried out. *"Jake! Get a grip!* I can't do this by myself; *please Jake!* She pleaded. It took another five minutes before he managed to regain some composure.

"Stay with Dane Jake, I'm going to call the ambulance and police."

Time seemed to stand still as she stood in front of the large bay window waiting for the police and ambulance. She heard the sirens in the distance, and her mouth instantly twisted into a cruel line. It had happened. Everything she had hoped for these past few years had finally been realized. Now her precious son could rest in peace. There was no doubt in her mind Dane had murdered Jeffrey, after all, the front door was still securely locked when they came home, and even though the laundry window next to the back door had been smashed to make it appear as a break in, any idiot could see it had been broken from the inside. Yes it was Dane alright, and as to why he would kill his brother, well only the devil knew, but for whatever reason, Dane would sit the rest of his life behind bars, and now her revenge was complete.

Jake sat in the kitchen in a mindless whirl of distortion and utter misery. One elbow placed casually on the table, supported his spinning head, his other arm hung limply beside. What was happening to him? What had he done that had been so bad during his life that warranted this kind of retribution and suffering? In the space of, how long, a few years he had lost all bar one of his children, who was now sitting mindless in the bedroom having gone through who knows what?

Had Dane witness the whole thing? Had he tried to stop the intruder, and now sat in a world of silence because he had failed? Or was he part of this abomination and has now gone made from guilt? He heard a soft voice in the distance and turned; Cassie was beside him; "The police are here Jake, you'd better pull yourself together, they'll want to ask questions."

He nodded and rose as Carl burst in, "*Where is he!?*" His voice was urgent yet professional; however, his red and puffy eyes betrayed his true emotions. "The bedroom," Jake whispered, then clearing his throat in an attempt to control his wavering voice, repeated louder, "The bedroom!"

Seconds later they heard Carl gasp, then a moment of silence before a series of not so polite adjectives spewed around the house in an extremely audible manner. "Son of a bitch!" he ended before turning to the young officers that had followed him in, "Get on the radio and see what's keeping forensic, I want this place dusted from to bottom, nothing is to be missed.

Cassie stood back, arms folded. The only fingerprints they would find would be theirs' and Danes'. It would be very interesting to see their faces once they realize who the 'son of a bitch' actually was, and she wouldn't miss it for the world.

Carl withdrew a notebook and pen from his pocket, "Alright Jake, let's have it from the top." The withered and broken man stared at his ex Father-in-law blankly; it was obvious he wasn't up to telling him anything. Cassie grabbed his visibly shaking hand and led him to a chair before and sighed; "I'm sorry Carl, I don't think Jake's up to speaking to you right now, but if I can help answer any questions please ask away.

"Yes alright Cassie; tell me what you know."

"We went to a party at around eight o'clock, the two boys were watching television when we left, and when we came home, well, we found Jeff's body; and Dane laying on Carly's bed in what seemed like a state of shock."

"I see. Did Dane tell you anything at all?"

She shook her head, "Like I said he seemed to be in shock. The only thing he said was "Why didn't they come for me, I waited, but they didn't come." And has just been staring into space ever since."

He sighed: "Alright. I'll see if I can get anything out of him. Have you had a look around the house; is anything missing, anything out of place?"

She shook her head, "No, when we came home the front door was still locked and everything was where it should be. In fact the only thing unusual was the fact the house was in darkness. We'd only been gone a couple of hours and still expected the boys to be watching the television. It was only the fact I heard the portable playing softly in the boys room, and Jake went to turn it off, that we found Jeffrey at all. Otherwise, we probably would have gone to bed and not noticed anything amiss until the morning.

It was only after Carl had left to question Dane, Cassie noticed the throng of people scurrying around the house. The Coroner had arrived along with forensic and two more squad cars, all unnoticed until now. She tip toed to the bedroom hoping to hear something interesting, but she needn't have bothered, because Dane was only repeating to his Grandfather what he had said to them. Then it happened, the moment she had been waiting for. A young constable pushed passed her and tapped Carl on the shoulder. He had been kneeling in front of Dane, and now rose and faced the young man. "Found something Roy?"

"Yes Sir." He cleared his throat before continuing, "It seems the laundry window was smashed with this," he held up a wooden statue, "However, the glass and statue were outside the house, indicating the glass was broken from the inside." Carl's face paled, "And, a partial trail of blood to the incinerator revealed this," he held up a plastic bag containing partly burned and bloodied clothes. Carl took the bag and looked over at Cassie, "Do you recognize these?" he swallowed the lump that threatened to choke him, and held it in front of her.

"Well, it's very difficult to say in that condition, but, the jeans look very similar to the ones we gave Dane for Christmas."

His ashen face stared at her for a very long time, there must be something wrong; it couldn't be. He turned to Dane, the lad was crying softly, "Are these your clothes Dane?"

Jake had entered unnoticed, and with new found courage laughed, "No, they are mine. I beheaded a few chickens some weeks ago, and didn't want Cassie to see the mess I'd made of my clothes, so I attempted to burn them. Guess I didn't light the damn thing properly." They all looked at him surprised, Roy coughed, "I don't think Mr. Marshall's memory is working to its' full capacity Serge. The incinerator was still smoldering.

It would seem the endeavor to burn them occurred tonight, not a few weeks ago.

Jake became extremely agitated, "Are you calling me a liar constable?"

"No sir, I merely suggested your memory to be a little bit confused."

Cassie came to his side and taking his hand gently, spoke softly, "Jake, it's no good. We both know there were no chickens, besides the blood on the garments will be tested, and whatever they find it to belong to, it certainly won't be hens."

Jake pushed her aside roughly, "Whose fucking side are you on!"

Jake, we know you are distraught, but Cassie is right, they will be tested," Carl reminded him harshly. He looked back at Dane, "Are these your clothes?" Tears were cascading down his face, he rose and stood before his stepmother, "Yes Grandpa, they belong to me, *BUT*, I didn't kill Jeffrey. I would never harm my own brother, I've been set up; *SHE* set me up." He had screamed that accusation at her and now grabbed her around the throat: "You're nothing but a *BITCH, a FUCKING BITCH!* Roy jumped forward and grabbed the youth by his shoulders, but he had found the strength of three men, and could not be moved. It took Carl and Jake's help before they could drag Dane from Cassie. She fell to the floor coughing and choking, her face was deathly grey.

Carl fought back the tears as he handcuffed his grandson, "I'm sorry Dane, I have to take you into custody, the charge; he faltered; "Is Murder"

Jake held his head and screamed *"NO! IT'S NOT TRUE!"*

Roy escorted Dane to the police car, and Carl turned to Cassie, his face creased with malice, "If Dane has been framed, *I WILL* find out, I promise you that." She smiled at him;

"Of course, and I sincerely hope you discover he has."

Epilogue

Carl sat in his unmarked police car in front of Rae's unit for a long time. His fingers strummed on the steering wheel furiously as he tried to collect his thoughts. It was all too simple. Dane wouldn't kill his own brother; it had to be a set up. But; how could he prove it? Cassie was his first suspect, yet she wasn't even there. She had to have been involved somehow, but how? He glanced at his daughter's front door. Not only did he have to tell her one of her sons had been murdered, he had to inform her, the other one has been arrested over it. Slowly he stepped from the car and made his way towards the portal.

He knocked several times before it opened slowly. Rae's face was masked with terror, her frail body covered by a thin cotton night gown, revealed protruding bones which not so long ago were covered evenly with flesh. "You've come to tell me something's happened to my boys, haven't you?"

She noted his swollen tear filled eyes averting her own, threw her head back and began to laugh hysterically, *"I KNEW IT, I KNEW IT!* Carly told me through the board, only about five hours ago; *Carly told me!"* Carl tried to embrace her, but she shunned his advances, ran to her easel and began ripping into the blank canvas with the knife she used for mixing the paints. As the wooden frame toppled to the floor, she ran to the sideboard like a woman possessed, picked up the small portable television and tossed it into the front window like a ball. Pieces of shard flew around the room like missiles, one missing Carl's face by millimeters. He tackled her in a rugby scrimmage, holding her tightly against his chest until hysteria lapsed into trembling sobs, then finally abated into a soft moan. He directed her into a chair, retreated into the small kitchenette and returned with a glass of brandy, "Here, drink this."

"I don't want it. I want to know the details"

"I think you should drink it Rae, it'll calm you down," he urged.

Closing her eyes from the burning tears, she made fists with her hands until the knuckles turned white and her palms bled from her long manicured nails digging into her flesh. She didn't want to be calm. Frustration and utter fury seethed within her veins, and she wanted to let go, she wanted to scream, and cry, and laugh. She wanted to grab her Father by the shoulders and shake him until his head hurt. She wanted to kill someone for taking her children … Jake … she wanted to kill Jake. Why wasn't he here with her, sharing her pain as before? He should be here, not home with that, that shrewish bitch of a woman. Somewhere from afar Carl's voice droned on, enticing her to drink, to drink … Within a split second she had reached out and knocked the glass from his hands, sending it hurtling through the air. *"I DON'T WANT THE DRINK! TELL ME WHAT HAPPENED!"* Even though she spoke softly, demurely, the words seemed to scream through her head like an tornado.

Carl looked at her bleeding hands, her vacant eyes and felt an eerie type of fear creep along his spine. She was at the edge, and he knew he was about to push her off. Somewhere in the back of his mind, something warned him to lie, to tell her Jeffrey was hurt but not seriously. That it had been a terrible accident and Dane had unintentionally stabbed him playing the goat. Yet he knew he couldn't. He couldn't alter the events of that night, no matter what repercussions may occur. Clearing his throat and kneeling before her, he took her hand gently, "Jeffrey was murdered tonight sweetheart." A soft, pitiful whimpering sound escaped from her throat, she took the corner of her lip between her teeth, and blood began to trickle down to her chin. Carl began to cry, he could feel her pain and his heart was breaking. It wasn't fair, it simply was not fair.

"I'm so sorry, my precious, I'm so sorry," he was sobbing. Rae took her Father's face between her hands and lifted his head to her, "That's not all, is it?"

Shaking his head slowly, he withdrew a handkerchief from his pocket and blew his nose, "I, I, oh boy!" he swallowed, "I had to arrest Dane for his murder."

Rae rose from her chair, she felt dizzy. *NO!* Screamed from behind her lips but no sound came. Bright lights flashed in front of eye, before she hit the ground and total darkness enveloped her.

Carl picked her up and placed her on the sofa; he was numb; void of feeling. He turned to leave and noticed the painting she had done of the children; uncovered leaning against the wall. He stared; Jeffrey had been removed from the birds' body and stood now with Carly and Felicity. But it was Dane that he couldn't take his eyes from; Dane's face was in the body of a bear, blood dripped from razor teeth and each claw held the head of Jake and Cassie.

THE END